THE
CHROMA

A NEW AGE WESTERN

A Novel by

ANSLEY RAY

go-go

HOUSE

THE CHROMA

2015 Go-Go House Trade Paperback Edition

Keywords: fiction, new age western, Forrest Fenn, Hopi Prophecy, Ansley Ray, Rainbow Warrior, Gordy Grundy, Aztec Treasure, Santa Fe,

Published in the United States of America

Book Publication and Design by Gordy Grundy

Portrait by Brett Colvin, www.BrettColvinPhotography.com

ISBN-13: 978-0692362488
ISBN-10: 0692362487
Library of Congress Control Number: 2015930485

HOUSE

www.GordyGrundy.com

Praise for THE CHROMA

"My eyes stayed glued to the words in this book until the candles burned low. The combination of hidden treasure and strong personalities kept this book in my hands long into the night. Ansley has a knack for putting words together that keeps her story flowing. Her words bring a drama to the page that won't let you stop reading. You just can't. I couldn't put this book down."
~ **Forrest Fenn**, Author and Treasure Impresario

"The book seemed very familiar, I felt a part of it. I have been to that portal."
~ **Charles Mills**, Elder and Founding Member of Rainbow Family of light

"*The Chroma* is jammed with history and adventure. Ansley has a story here that will make you think and keep you up at night. This is good old fashioned fun."
~ **Dal Neitzel**, Treasure Hunter

"*The Chroma* is awesome!"
~ **Rattlesnake**, Rainbow Elder

"The Aztec called it *teocuitlatl*, which means "excrement of the gods." Partly lore, partly fact, this precious, glistening metal has lured generations of people to seek its beauty and value as if an invisible hand possesses and involuntarily pulls its seekers, promising riches that lie just out of touch, but within reach in their fevered and focused minds. However, discovery and possession is as fleeting as finding one's own identity, our purpose in this world.

Praise for THE CHROMA

What is driving Rain's passion? Is it her voyage to discover herself and her demons or is it truly the thrill of the chase – perhaps it is both! The treasure that Rain discovers during this journey is inestimable. It lies buried within everyone with a will to survive and a heart filled with love and forgiveness. And it just might be the power of an Aztec gold bracelet that calls to Rain to seek her treasure.

~ **Randy S. Cameron**, Batman

"Beyond the wild redhead on a souped-up racing bike, buried treasure, the Hopi Prophecy, a Mothership and a chase across the Southwest, *The Chroma* is also a very sensitive story of a woman coming to terms with her history of abuse. The struggle is honest and deeply expressed."

~ **Marion Delgado**, Author

"It is about getting a message out about the Rainbow Family, about our prophecy, and how we are portrayed and what We really are. This book takes you on a journey through time and our history and legacy."

~ **Rainbow Elder Irvin**

"An enticing and emotional story of a woman whose life challenges bring her closer to her most intimate self. Rain reminds all of us that no matter how hard the journey, the powers of Gaia and the protectors of the universe are always present when we are ready to truly see. The Chroma is an expression of great wonders and reminds the reader of the magical and mystical powers in this world that still exist today."

~ **Emilee**, Rainbow Warrior and Potion Maker

FOREWORD

As an editor and publisher, my goal is to illuminate the author in the very best light and composition. Writer Ansley Ray provoked much consideration as she is a writer of thought and emotion as well as style.

I am very proud of the effort. Special editorial and visual attentions were placed upon her unique and poetic cadence and avant garde line breaks. She writes with design and courage.

Ray has created a true New Age Western. *The Chroma* is a phantasmagoric epic. I believe in the work and integrity of Ansley Ray. Her wild spirit and hope are enviable.

To answer two common questions:

1) Yes, there are important clues and insights to the Forrest Fenn adventure in this book.

2) Yes, there is a puzzle in *The Chroma* and it yields a very valuable and personal treasure.

I shall say no more about any of it.

~ Gordy Grundy

AUTHOR'S NOTE

Inspired by seeds of truth, my own quest for the chest and a struggle for answers to health, "The Chroma" is from my heart. *The Thrill of the Chase* by Forrest Fenn exists. Mr. Fenn, a supportive friend, is a delightful and talented writer. He hid a treasure worth millions for anyone willing to look. *The Thrill of the Chase* inspired my story and sparked a desire to continue life. I was blessed to meet him in my quest and I am thrilled to have his thumbs up for this story.

His treasure is north of Santa Fe and his character in this book has been made up. Several other fictional tales have been written about Forrest and his chest, but I wanted to be bold and use his name, as it is a great one. Thank you Forrest Fenn!

A small word of caution, please. Listen only to what he wrote or said if you are looking for the box. Forrest is very private and has already left the answers.

Hot Springs, Montana and the lore of the Dragon below the mountain are true, but this story and all characters within are a product of my imagination. Happy hunting. Remember to look inside!

Many thanks to our Creator for giving us a chance. Thanks to all of those who have supported this endeavor!

To Gaia and Her infinite patience with humankind's growth process; I have faith.

To my son, for inviting expanded imagination, to those who inspired the dreams and visions, to Forrest Fenn for sparking a thrilling adventure, the seed of my story, to beginnings and endings, and to those who hung in and waited for me to arrive! Thanks to Brett Colvin photography for the dreams, ideas and pictures. To Irvin and family, I love you!

Breathe in, breathe out, that is IT...

Let us awaken to our purpose, Light Warriors

"Awaken out of the dream of time into the presence."
~ Eckhart Tolle, *The Power of Now*

~ Ansley Ray

THE

CHROMA

THE
CHROMA

CHAPTER I

TIME

"Happiness is a journey not a destination."

Buddha

"Crap!"

The fiery redhead shouted.

An enormous mule deer jumped into the middle of the misty Blue Slide Road.

She slammed on the brakes, leaving a long skid.

The buck bounced off through the thick brush, then through the forest.

"That was blooming close." Rain said to her enormous, black and white

shaking dog.

She watched the buck, fading into memories that brought her close to her

edge.

Rain, her name since she left this place, was shaking herself.

It had been long enough, she thought, but her system was flooded with rage. Spring Creek

Community brought up her issues. Took her out of the now.

Here, in the same spot, thirty years earlier, or so, the van slid on the ice coming close to plunging into Vermillion Creek.

Angie, the staff driver, had just chuckled.

"Well, it would not be the first swim in here."

The kids just stared at each other, silently accepting what was beyond their control.

During warm months a jump from the Vermillion Bridge into the icy river made everything

better.

Spring Creek frowned on it, but some staff had stopped anyway, for the thrill.

Her survival group had jumped all at once.

"One, two, three jump!" Eileen hollered, watching for cars.

The group had needed a good lift.

Smiling, they scrambled out.

Memories of the survival and challenger courses, the school and feelings flooded.

Taking her to places she had purposely forgotten.

Traveling the Blue Slide was coming full circle, back to roots that were forced to grow, sliced

and pushed into the ground.

It was here, in Thompson Falls, Montana, that Rain learned about quiet.

Solitude.

She had spent almost five days alone, in the wilderness, two nights had been without a

fire.

Rain carried few possessions, traveling with her giant dog, Dasher.

The weight of holding up the world had finally bent her to a snapping point.

She was giving it all up.

Running from more than herself.

The adrenaline pumped through her nervous veins toward a hurried destination, sweaty and cold.

Down the dilapidated lane, the decaying remnants of Spring Creek, lay empty and full of memories and lingering ghosts.

Rain had driven up and walked around the vacant buildings, ignoring the private property

signs. Her blood, sweat and tears gave her every right to be there.

Rain left a small treasure from her pouch as an offering.

"I release these negative thoughts, feelings and associations about my time here. Please

take them from me," Rain begged.

Leaving, she felt the heaviness of the collective pain surrounding the softly scented pines and meadows.

Voices still echoed, emptily around the dorms and kitchen.

After a long last look, Rain gunned it out down the potholed lane.

She rolled down the windows and let the crisp air freshen her mood. She gasped at the

cold blast and turned the music up.

Her moods and temper had caused great controversy. Spring Creek had been the solution.

"I cannot believe that place has not burned down."

"Maybe, I should."

Thought better of it.

She sighed and looked at how the town had grown, carefully rolling through at 23 mph.

The Black Bear, Little Bear and Minnie's were still there, but a health food store and a few fancy buildings had popped up, and a new bar and grill. Thompson Falls bustled.

It was up and coming now.

Changes welcomed by a starving community.

Driving on, with the wind blowing her long, wavy, flame-licked hair into frenzied whips around her still wet face, she let out a low howl that the hungry wind swallowed with thirsty gulps.

Letting the elements soothe her as the music blasted on. A flute hammered into her soul with gentle taps of drums.

Turning it up, the music was a salve.

The sting lessened, healing seeping in.

It had been good to look.

Satisfaction with the empty abandonment felt gleefully wrong.

Spring Creek and its ghosts were an obstacle for her.

Rain needed to let go and was getting close.

Rain was making the powers nervous.

She was too close to important answers, knew too much.

Rain was on her way home.

A town where outlaws, artists, tourists, cowboys, indians, locals and hippies roamed the town stuck fifty years behind. Hot Springs, Montana.

It suited her perfectly.

People came for hiding and healing in Hot Springs.

The pace was on Indian time, a vortex unlike others that swirled.

Google Maps showed a heart and those who could see the energy saw a green bridge over the town.

There was not a cell tower in sight. There were those that had not even touched a computer due to a righteous suspicion and an understanding of how technology was controlling the human mind.

Rain had driven over her cell phone, repeatedly, in Wyoming, backing over it one last time, just to be sure.

Taking her tracking device out of it, she stuck it on a truck with South Carolina plates.

She knew they would find her, but it was amusing to think of the scramble.

Rain was picking up a different shadow that required more than getting rid of the technology.

She shivered, as a cool wind touched her neck, thinking of the monsters.

The creatures that created the drama, to take Gaia.

Rain sensed them.

Heard tiny whispers and warnings, deep within, she just knew.

Go forward and look remained her only choice.

Her grandmother had left her a small couple of lots, just below the H Mountain.

Hoping she would return in time, unable to physically be there with her, protecting from above.

She was alone, except for the Watchers.

Rain felt the lurking presence.

A chill behind her neck.

Watched, but if she knew how closely, it would bother her, so they stayed back, fighting a silent battle and protecting as much as possible.

Rain's Guardians had their work cut out for them, part of an old agreement.

The highest trained watchers and protectors had been assigned a duty.

The implications were beyond imagination and human understanding.

They agreed to sacrifice a living body to be able to watch from the realms of spirits, calling on an ancient and true Source.

The challenges, set before this life, were the most difficult yet.

Rain knew it, her exhalation would be complete rest in the Waters of home, she had to get centered and healthy, more to depended on it than she could imagine.

Hot Springs had the second highest mineral content in the world.

Travelers came from all over to heal.

Without returning to the beginning, Rain would never finish finding the answers she sought so hard.

Barely making it out of Salt Lake City alive, she, at least, was now on the right track.

Sagiditis, the enemy of Gaia, knew it would hunt her and figure out her role.

The story had been painful, but one she was coming to know as home, regardless of the reminders of the trials on the trails.

Rain had come to understand more and more about choices and the consequences of them.

She had chosen dangerously but it was beyond her control, a destiny gratefully taken on.

Rain was a warrior of the Light, a truth bringer, a carrier of the old bloodlines so protected, a descendant of Mary Magdalene and Jesus.

Part of the biggest cover up yet.

On the council of the Atlantean Task and the Universal Peace Force and as a Universal Law Bringer and Upholder, Rain was bound by an ancient contract to protect this planet.

So far, it was a mess.

Humans were losing ground on a daily basis. Tons of chemicals were sprayed. The ground was hammered and split open. Entire mountains removed. People were killing, raping, pillaging and showing a general lack of evolution of the heart.

The mind disease, fed by greed, was taking Gaia, poisoning the air and water and tricking millions.

Layers of fog and sickness hid the answers.

It kept the humans asleep.

Enslaved.

Happily entranced and asleep, from the poisons and the controlling waves from the electronic devices.

They continued to work blindly, feeding a perpetual system designed to build wealth for just a few.

The quest had ancient roots.

Her part vital to the survival of the planet.

A spell had been placed upon her, lifetimes ago.

Memory chips implanted by the Ancient Council.

Reagan was awakening.

Each memory brought layers of pain and freedom.

This was not the first time her people had fought for a planet.

The Task Force traveled the galaxy and defended it.

On call, ready, always to help as

warriors of Light.

Ever holding the mirror to the dark.

The fight for territory was increasing. The small beautiful planet had been targeted by a vicious population of intergalactic, outlawing thieves.

Her own Star people had fought them off and vowed to watch and protect.

Gaia was too important, universally, to be lost.

Hope for humankind diminished, the few left held deeply.

The Planet needed help.

It was Gaia Herself that held the value.

Giant Crystals, designed as communication and portal devices, rested on Her.

The balance of the Universe teetered on the Awakening of the Humans.

Rain did not remember everything, but had heard the whispers behind her back, and knew she played an important role.

Rattles shook when her name was called. People whispered.

So far, she was struggling to remember and go forward. She had given herself these challenges to overcome on purpose, to be ready.

Rain was strong and wildly beautiful. She had studied many arts.

Spent her life struggling and learning to overcome the challenges and pain.

She saw, felt deeply and maintained her ability to communicate with animals and angels.

She had been taught and given tools that she was only now seeing and understanding.

Rain had begun her travels and studies after leaving Spring Creek.

Going first to Hawaii, Reagan had changed her name and started her training in earnest.

Training, in one-way or another, had become part of her story.

Each lifetime specifically designed to bring her right here.

The challenges had been difficult.

Her life almost lost.

Precious time wasted.

She earned belt after belt and changed directions to study as many forms as she could.

She learned to meditate, breathe and work energy.

She learned to pray to the Creator daily and to be thankful for every breath.

Rain knew she would heal, if she stayed grounded, if she went home and if she could resist the threats against her.

She was running.

Running fast and hard for life and for the lives of all beings on the planet.

She studied, hid, healed and searched.

She had to find the box before anyone else did.

It was a matter of life and death for the whole planet.

The Universe needed this planet.

Rain was not alone in her quest to save Her.

It was well known to the enemy who Reagan Bauer really was.

They had to keep her running and sick, or she would find out that the whispers were true.

CHAPTER II

HISTORY

"When the Earth is ravaged and the animals are dying, a new tribe of people shall come unto the Earth from many colors, creed and classes and who by their actions and deeds shall make the Earth green again. They shall be known as Warriors of the Rainbow."

Hopi Prophecy

Rain came from mixed blood and was considered an outsider from both sides, Native American and blue blooded Aryan European, a Métis.

They were furious with her mother for marrying into her Father's Ute bloodline.

Her Mother's father, Adolf Bauer, had taken out his prejudices on her again and again.

Rain fumed at the thought of him and breathed out a dark cloud of the resentment, bristling at an idea she needed to let go, that she had to be the one to move forward.

First, she had to uncover some deeply buried lies.

Her stomach swirled as she thought of the prejudices she was to face.

"Dasher, boy, nobody likes a hard truth."

He panted.

She knew she was holding the mirror, bringing up deeply seeded pain and anger.

The prophecies of the secrets of the Seven Cities of Cibola, lying in Mormon hands, were built upon the lies of the most ancient dark out there, an alien one.

Gold was a gift from the great Mother Dragon, and held the key to magical powers of transforming dark energy into Light.

Gaia's magic.

Aliens have been letting the humans mine, collect and pile it, conveniently.

Soon Sagiditis planned on taking off, in their ships, with all of the gold.

Humans had been tricked into slavery.

The Tribes were not immune, blaming white and western influence kept feeding shadow, not changing.

Rain had to get through.

The Tribes were felt to be immune to the greed disease and most continued to allow the government to poison them with bad food. They maintained an attitude of victimhood.

Well, the planet was falling apart, as far as Rain had seen on the Reservations. The "Earth People" had been tricked too, participating just as much.

Many lived in addiction, diabetes and the continued attitude of having been wronged, but not doing anything about it, because of the mind games and control the government maintained on them.

Trickery ran rampant, Western influence in the farthest corners.

The pieces of the trickery puzzle were lining up, ready to be put together.

The Tribes, all of them, needed to stand up, refuse the poison and fight for Gaia.

Unite, as One People, under Gaia, indivisible through Love.

The power needed to be awakened and all to admit their own wrong doings and lack of protection.

It was time to unplug.

The alien ships hovered, invisible.

Waiting.

Plotting.

Watching.

Spreading clouds of confusion, cutting light webs woven together.

Cutting out obstacles.

Rain was getting in the way.

All humans were under control, tricked.

It had been carefully planned and executed, how to enslave the Light Beings.

"We be they slaves, yes we be, boy." Rain roughed the dog's fur.

Secrets lying deeply buried, only symbols remain.

Many find themselves studying symbols, realizing this trap, humans walked into, was not too late to see.

"Everywhere you go, boy, they watch you."

An ever seeing eye stared at you, symbols meant to distract and scramble apart the collective consciousness.

Cameras were on every corner, satellites, data mining, monitoring, spying, watching every move.

Easy to fix, hard to get there.

As soon as one breath was taken together in Love, humans could be rid of the forces, getting the fog to lift long enough for this pause in time to happen, nearly impossible.

A quick pause in time.

Time out.

Labels, divisions, languages, colors, sexes, teams, countries, clothing, styles, ways to identify our mind disease controlled the vast majority of collective hearts.

Words were used to confuse.

Rewritten, played with, to manipulate.

Words and weapons, carrying a vibration.

Playing a tune to control brain waves.

Language, music to soothe or bang around clanging with echoes of pain. Powerful magic, easy to use to control massive amounts of people.

The Bible had been edited to be convenient, using the kind and open-hearted gullibility and propensity for wrong choices and lessons, as a tool to control and bring darkness.

The very righteous usually were the first to slam the door on the beggar or the whore, thereby ignoring the simple teachings of Christ.

They had killed him for his message.

Love one another, God is within, so when you love each other, you are loving God.

Anything else is the same.

People kept sinning on the free will planet.

The message was blocked.

People were on the wrong road, blindly walking into a trap set.

The gold was mounded high in caverns and in the treasuries.

Brokers had been placed everywhere to collect the precious metal.

It was about to be vacuumed up, stolen.

Humans had mined it, greedily piling it, listening to the rampant lies designed to keep the truth hidden from our hearts.

Now, it was about to be taken, forever.

She could not live without it.

Alchemy.

The old quest.

The unrest grew.

War, famine, drought, wildfires, floods, darkness and strife winning.

"Dasher, dear friend, we have to get people to see in the mirror, before it is too late."

Rain interrupted her musings to check in with the overly large black and white dog that had found her in Salt Lake.

Dasher had leapt in her car nine months before.

Rain needed him.

He gratefully had picked the huge body and appeared before her car, at just the right time.

"Phew boy, things are a mess. Man, did you feel that?" Rain shivered as the shadow crossed over the car.

Within her, answers lay waiting.

Stripping the distractions layered, Rain could clearly see into the heart of dark, knowing it too needed to be seen, felt and loved anyway.

Though Rain knew seeing would be hard, the recent changes in the Earth had the Elders and multiple levels of the Councils worried enough.

Her family had transplanted from the Southern Ute lands in the early 1900's and now lived near Flathead Lake. They were part of a multi-tribal secret council directly linked to the Ancient Magical Timeless and Universal Peace Council.

She had not spoken to most of her family for a long time.

They had struggled to accept her, but there were those who knew she could do this.

She struggled to overcome her resentments and accept her role.

It was told.

It had been prophesied that Rain was to bring about the awakening for the changes needed to save Gaia, the living, breathing planet, she called home in this life.

She was to carry out an important mission, risking herself.

For years, the angelic Council watched, waited and hoped she would be ready.

Well, she was ready now.

Her return meant the beginning of the new.

If this were to be a continued cycle of dark, nobody was sure Gaia would come through, even without humans or aliens abusing Her.

Times were desperate.

Heating up.

Literally.

The planet rested on a delicate wire, ready to fall into either side of the edge.

They gathered and discussed.

The Council decided to send a physical representative to be there to watch, to help.

He was called, Dasher.

CHAPTER III

EXPLORATIONS

"And the end of all of our exploring
Will be to arrive where we started
And know the place for the first time."

T.S. Eliot

Checking her mirrors and keeping her senses heightened, being sure to be extra cautious, Rain let the river's changing currents run through her.

Feeling herself relax, she sipped some Gem potion, needing to refresh her invisibility, to keep them off her energy trail.

Softening, melting into time and space, simply seeing, breathing, being.

She had stopped in Missoula, to see a friend, an alchemist.

Nita refreshed her herbs, magic potions and crystals.

From birth, Nita trained to be a Medicine Woman aware of multiple layers of energy, able to heal and protect on all levels.

Extraordinary for a healer.

Usually working in one or two realms, only.

"You be safe and well, walk in Light and Love, Sister. The one in the purple vial might be especially useful right now. Take a few drops when you sense you need to blend into your environment. I have been having visions of an old world and of some danger you might be in. I sense you will get to where you are going, if you can stay where you are."

She hugged Rain and floated off in a trail of Frankincense and Rose, her long purple robe snapping gently along behind her.

Exiting Butterfly Herbs, Rain stepped onto Higgins Street.

Fresh air blew, from the storm that rolled through the night before.

Cleansing, cool.

The air felt so good, Rain about missed the cyclist barreling down the bike lane.

"Look out!"

He glared at her, splashing through a small puddle.

"Wow, wake up." She thought to herself and him.

Puzzling still, she looked both ways before crossing to her VW.

Rain wondered, but knew it would make sense when she needed it to.

Making it through the congestion of Reserve and out 93, her heart began to flutter.

Home and history were close.

Her eyes stared deeply ahead as she pulled off Highway 200.

"I can't believe where we are Dasher, look at this, I love this road, this river means home to me."

Fall was coming.

Colors shifted into reds, yellows and brilliant orange.

The smooth, swift Flathead, deeply blue green, ran hurriedly alongside.

Snow capped the Mission Mountains, already.

The huge black and white dog grinned.

His head out the window, lapping the fresh air.

He had not liked Salt Lake City.

He had worried about his charge.

She was sick.

Dasher could only barely keep the long trail of oozing dark off her.

He could feel and smell her getting better.

When he sniffed her ears now, he barely smelled the rolling emotions and fear.

The sick smell was leaving.

His tongue hung and he rested with the wind blowing through his silken fur.

Rain felt a twinge in her belly.

A fluttery, nervous, beat against her ribs.

It was here she had met him, the one man who had long ago stolen her heart.

She had stopped thinking of him so much.

Rain wished the clues were not bringing her home.

Where she would have to think of him.

She could hear his silvery and contagious laugh booming in her mind.

He had practically run her over, she laughed.

"Now, wouldn't that be something. I have not seen him in a long time, my sweet puppy dog friend. He be not for me anyway." Scratching his ears, she sang off key, making it up.

"Darn it, how did I get on that?"

She was not to let this distraction cloud her mission.

Breathing in a cloak, she let it surround her field.

Thoughts of him could ease her into dark emotions quickly.

She knew, the twinge in her belly was emotions needing to be let go of and allowing them to breed would signal her location.

"There, that ought to hold them long enough for to me to look around here again."

Most of the time, she had an invisible tail.

Lately they had gotten bolder and had appeared in the physical realm.

Wisps of dark.

Glimpses of Shadow in her side-views.

She saw the tail of something disappear, when she really looked.

Above the planet, the Serpent Queen, Shankar, hissed out her frustration, as she sensed Rain hiding herself, finding what she needed.

"How the Hell did this peon escape Salt Lake City? The death potion I brewed should kill at least two nasty Light Workers?"

"Her magic must be stronger again."

"We have to beat her to the town. She cannot find the Chroma and unlock the doors to the Dragon's Chambers."

"All of the old magic is hidden there."

"If she does, we need to be waiting, or the whole of this damn few hundred years will be for nothing. Our ship goes back to the Void, if that stupid Chroma box gets opened."

"Watch her!" Shankar hissed low and slow.

"Keep her twisted in time, locked in her shadows."

"Yes, my Queen." The serpentine servant bowed.

Left to carry out orders.

Rain had found eight objects, in different locations, thousands of miles apart, leading her home, here.

Seeing her favorite place in the mirror reflected as the objects danced in front of a mirror, the Flathead River caverns.

A beautiful figure rose, doing intricate movements, breathing in a rhythmic pattern.

Music floated, as words appeared and drifted off.

Then at the cavern, it stopped.

A doorway was locked.

The key, a mirror of another.

Something else was needed here.

She wanted to see what was inside.

Hopefully, the Chroma.

Bronze, beautiful, full of mystery, life and millions.

Her Grandmother told her legends about this portal.

This had to be it. This is where Forrest put it.

How tricky.

The illusive, bronze, Romanesque lock box held treasures beyond time and space.

Items meant to open portals to locked up mysteries and magic.

Hidden, by her people, lifetimes ago.

Rain glanced behind, took the left hand turn driving down the bumpy dirt road, hopeful and excited, in disbelief at being there.

The small black car bouncing, navigating around the puddles and rocks with ease.

She loved the deep blue green tint of the water and admired an extra large red tail hawk circling the field.

Colored leaves blew off the cottonwoods, starting the winter blanket.

It was good to be home.

When she reached the line of rocks hiding a cavern, she pulled the E brake, hopped out.

Dasher ran after a rabbit.

Rain stretched.

Taking in the big ponderosas and the swift currents, she let the memories flood.

Rumors had been spoken of.

Long ago, Rain overheard conversations about a series of hidden caverns, containing answers and magic, well hidden.

She had been coming to this place forever.

Her Grandmother sat with her under the huge ponderosas, cottonwoods, sharing creation stories from before the time of now.

A threat had come.

The People hid answers.

She ran her hands along the edges by the ancient pictographs.

It was within these walls that the box must lay resting, waiting to tell.

A bead of sweat trickled down her neck making a chill settle to her toes.

The Chroma, deeply reflective of self.

It was hard to remember.

The programming had been good.

She placed her hands on the stone, held her amulet, now thick and lumpy, and watched it glow and begin shift.

She found the clues left behind in eight places the poem fit, each one bringing her closer to here.

Rain baffled the puzzle was dragging her home.

She never wanted to come back here.

Her issues surrounding her past swallowed the present.

Moving ahead, harder here.

Facing the demons, necessary.

Eight times thinking she had found the chest, another clue came.

In her dreams, they told her she would look for this and she had laughed.

"Is she ready yet?"

"No way, she does not even listen."

"The key, the key, she needs the key."

Rain awoke lying at the base of the rocks.

What happened?

She had been looking for the entrance.

She had dreamed of another time.

She had needed a key to get in the cavern.

Where was this key? Why had the poem led her here?

"Darn it," she cussed, and then caught herself.

"Oh, sorry."

Rain collected her temper.

Breathing slow.

Filling her lungs.

Inviting energy in.

Breathing out anything not needed.

Out it whooshed.

She brushed off the leaves and dirt and absentmindedly wandered to her shiny black 1965 bug.

Freshly painted, with a sunroof cut.

The interior original, pristine.

A steal from an estate sale, the year before.

It started with a small sputtering protest, quickly humming and purring.

Rain knew how to care for cars.

She liked this little Volkswagen, babied it.

Putting thousands into refurbishing it.

It was fully loaded.

Rain ran her hands over the dragon she had just found in Wyoming, smoothly marbled burnt red.

Cool to the touch, a sweet power contained within, it chimed.

Heading up the last thirty miles of road to Hot Springs, she let the car run a couple times.

The road was empty, too tempting.

When the speedometer reached 100, she slowed again.

The red signs announcing the local businesses were a bit distracting.

Usually there was a speed trap ahead, anyway.

Hot Springs Lumber, Hot Springs Fitness, Syme's, Loafin' Around, Alameda's, Buck's, Fergie's, they flashed by, begging tourists to stop.

Rain was irritated and road weary, annoyed to be empty-handed.

Excited to see home.

She liked finding something when searching.

She did not care what.

Today, Rain felt she lost.

Not sure what the land would look like, Rain drove forward, slower.

It had an outhouse, a tipi and a shed, but not much else.

She needed a soak, so figured she would drop her stuff and then head over to the Waters.

Pulling into town, the local sheriff was parked in his usual spot, by the Corner Store, waiting for someone to speed through. Rain waved.

He looked puzzled and then excited.

She had stirred lots of trouble up as a teen, he remembered her and thought back fondly to several incidents with Rain and a local boy that she dated, on the lookout hill.

He had gotten a good view of her adolescent body and was embarrassed at his response then and now.

He had not been able to stop thinking of her, when he drove by the hill, wanted to see her again.

He made a mental note to drop by later.

The Council gathered above.

Meeting in the ancient Medicine Wheel, they sat at a Round Table.

Words were not needed.

They would be meeting daily, meditating, watching.

Rain pulled into the lot admiring the two large willows.

Her tipi stood between, and looked OK, on this side.

Considering how long she had been gone, relief flowed into her system.

Rain was tired.

Needed rest.

The damage was minimal and the mice had not gotten in the fire supplies or basics in the storage shed.

She was able to get set up, with a steaming gourd of Yerbe Mate, in just ten minutes.

Stashing her small pack, Rain picked up her books, glanced longingly at the chest in the picture.

She was ready to soak and shed some of the mental garbage that had accumulated.

Setting *The Thrill of the Chase*, with all of the notes in her tipi, she headed to the Symes Hotel.

CHAPTER IV

THE THRILL

"As I have gone alone in there
And with my treasures bold,
I can keep a secret where,
And hint of riches new and old.
Begin it where warm waters halt
And take it in the canyon down,
Not far, but too far to walk.
Put it in below the home of Brown.
From there it's no place for the meek,
The end is ever drawing nigh,
There'll be no paddle up your creek,
Just heavy loads and water high.
If you have been wise and found the blaze,
Look quickly down, your quest to cease,
But tarry scant with marvel gaze,

Just take the chest and go in peace.

So why is it that I must go

And leave my trove for all to seek?

The answers I already know,

I've done it tired, and now I am weak.

So hear me all and listen good,

Your effort will be worth the cold.

If you are brave and in the wood

I give you title to the gold."

Forrest Fenn

The Thrill of the Chase

A beautiful bronze box, Romanesque, locking, and filled with treasures old and new, had been hidden.

Supposedly North of Santa Fe, in the Rocky Mountains, anyone could look.

Just needing the nine clues contained in one of Forrest Fenn's books, *The Thrill of the Chase*.

Rain had been looking for a year now.

The Thrill of the Chase, saving her from a dark depression and motivating her to get well.

Though her trail was the hottest, and as each day ticked by, more searchers began to look.

Some with motivation beyond treasure hunting.

The Chroma, the alchemical power of transforming dark into light, it held within, had been hidden for centuries and protected by the Ancient Peace Keeping, Universal Task Force.

The power within had caused the downfall of other worlds, in different times, on this spinning blue world.

The magic had attracted the Serpentine aliens, Sagiditis.

The chest once held the original scriptures written by Mary and Jesus, both.

The instructions meant to be carried out.

How it should have been.

Humans had been hiding and guarding it since these greedy creatures had shown up several hundred years earlier.

The magic it held, too important.

"Dasher, the People need to see Truth again! Can they deal?"

She hoped the people were ready for it, finally, as the planet was in dire need.

Rain hoped it was not too late.

The planet was gasping Her last breaths, just being held by a few brave and weary souls, still fighting.

Poverty predominant in the mindset of greed and consumerism.

Long ago, her people had foreseen the devastation coming, hidden many secrets and placed advanced chips and blocks in the souls, both reminding and protecting information at the same time.

It was said they were to dissolve slowly, during this critical time.

Many of the warriors had been killed, were ill or had fallen prey to the distractions so carefully placed.

Even the tribe, supposedly to save the planet, was caught up in a fantasy designed to continue to keep them in the dark, though they felt enlightened. They still were spinning.

Just to be safe, her people had planned on this.

"Hey, hey doggie, I love you." She stopped her train-wrecked thoughts and sang to the dog.

Rain had been one of the many leaders.

In this life she was to be an outsider, hard to like, going through many challenges.

This kept her able to see.

Rain needed to be able to help awaken the ancient heart fires born from the Mother of all Dragons.

The Chakra System of the Mother Dragon ran from Montana down to New Mexico.

All the way down to the tail, at Ojo Caliente and Jemez.

The pools collected, filtered and returned energy.

She rested in the waters, waiting, protected, glorious in her beauty, breathing the fire of life.

Her breath was the water in the Springs.

The evidence in the healing.

Humans, or most of them did not see how the water really looked, and what it took away.

Only the ancient Atlantean bloodline was able to awaken the Mother Dragon, Ahomea, the bringer of Light, the Awakener.

This secret had been deeply buried and protected on both sides, just as her mixed bloodlines had caused conflict in this lifetime, the key to the question being hidden in the heart was unlocked.

Unlocking the doors took multiple keys.

Otherwise it would be too easy.

She had to get here first.

The big dog lapped up the attention and wordlessly agreed.

"Yes, they needed to hurry."

"I love you too." He beamed at her.

She had found the cavern near her home reflected when placing all eight objects uncovered beside a mirror.

She had placed them there randomly, surprised at the image reflecting.

Dancing figures gracefully and anciently opened a portal.

It was a wall of pictographs, near her home in Montana.

She had driven ten thousand miles and thought she had the chest eight times, but only found interesting and powerful objects.

It was a one of the finest puzzles ever imagined, with live keys to unlocking the next clues.

All tiny replicas of treasures in the Chroma or indicative somehow. Rain wondered if the last place was truly where the chest rested, or another tempting tease.

Her mouth watered thinking about having her hands on the treasure.

Rain could feel the gold and jewels sliding through her hands.

The view was dark.

The chest was dirty.

Her nerves wired even imagining.

The ties between what she had overheard about herself, as a child, and this quest were starting to bother her.

She never thought she could bring the change they spoke of her bringing and had not started looking for this treasure to save anyone but herself. She had been feeling so sick, and thought if she found it, she could, at least rest and enjoy the last of her time.

It had reminded her of the night she dreamed about the Council, talking of her, or more like arguing.

"Reagan Bauer cannot be the Truth Bringer. She is too emotional to See."

"It already is spoken, she will have to overcome."

It went on, in the dream.

She could feel the ancient voices and knew maybe she did have a deep calling.

The more she looked for the bronze chest, the more she knew it was somehow related.

Her stomach roiled in fear, she was falling, and fast.

This weight both lifted and sunk her.

She knew that all of it had a purpose.

Every last challenge and tear.

Every time she learned to rise above, she did just that and affected change she did not understand.

She had searched far and wide and in eight places had discovered a tiny magical item related to the chest.

Well-hidden, but full of hope and motivation, the objects had an energy together.

Each discovery involved several blazes, be it a mark in a tree, or a pile of stones. Forrest Fenn's blazes are subtle. One had to line them up in the right light.

The objects were bulky now, in her overstuffed pouch.

The weight was comfortable, hanging around her neck.

Heavy by nightfall, she had taken to placing it on the shelf.

One evening, the shelf rested before an antique mirror.

The objects moved, sung, then shape-shifted into the view of the caverns.

It had been one of her favorite places to go as a child.

Her Grandmother had taken her there often.

This is where she had learned about her family's ancient magic and had been gifted the tools to go with it.

Grandmother Sun Bear had been killed before Rain's training

had been completed.

Rain had lost all desire to learn, fell into horrible mood swings and rebelled at the idea of being herself.

Rain knew it had been no accident.

Her grandmother had been gathering herbs by Dog Lake.

They had only found her shawl and some blood spatters.

The case was still open, one of her major challenges.

"Dasher, I still dream of the Shadow that swallowed her." Shivering, a tear slid down her face.

Her grandmother had always been there, and had been the one to comfort her after her Grandfather Bauer finished mopping up his needs with her young body.

She taught Rain to fly, to go to different lands, reminded her of great magic and purpose, told her of a sleeping Dragon waiting for her.

The tales had kept her alive; she did not know, then, the truth of it.

CHAPTER V

WAKE UP CALL

"Liberate them, do the dance of self, to what tune do you dance, what magic do you perform, push consciousness to a new height, work together as teams, like rays coming out from the spirals of the Central Sun, awaken the intelligence inside, you are renegade members of the Family of Light, system busters, on call, available to bust up dark systems Universally, your assignment is to awaken a spark of Light. Family of Light, wake up! See with ancient eyes. Activate your memories. Take it back, free the enslaved humans with a revolution of consciousness. You are here to save the world."

Paraphrased from Pleiadan Message for 2012,
A Wake Up Call

She was just dreaming, she thought.

The men following her, she had ditched with a few easy evasive tactics.

Rain was not the only one looking for this answer within the Chroma.

There were those seeking to destroy it and anyone close to it.

The answers within were too profound.

Several parties followed her every movement.

She had alien forces, the law, an ancient Council with her.

She really was never alone.

The law was losing interest, as they could never find anything wrong, but then they were patient.

Rain was careful.

They were the new ones.

She was used to being watched.

They had seen her every movement, heard her every thought, her whole life.

They waited.

Some not very patiently.

She was pretty good at hiding, at least for long enough to escape real danger. She lived on the edge of it all of the time, though, and was unaware of the true implications of her success or failure.

The balance of the Universe rested with this time.

The impatient watchers threw obstacles and inserted thoughts whenever she was absent from her body, making it harder for her to stay centered.

If Reagan Bauer knew who she was, she would be frightened.

So, they watched and waited, cheering and leering.

Recently, in the century that they were in, the Chroma had been hidden by Forrest Fenn, now legendary for *The Thrill of the Chase*.

He placed several ancient artifacts that carried alchemy and the box itself held ancient and protected secrets, hoped by some, to have been destroyed.

If the magic within the chest were let into the hearts of the humans, then Gaia would win.

According to law, She would be left alone and returned to the rightful owners.

The end of the human slavery and return to living lovingly, peacefully and in the Light intended.

What the searchers were not aware of, or some of them, was the deeper implication of this chest.

It would be hard to find in the current dimension, it rested in another reality, reflecting itself.

The reality was the one in legends, the ones spoke by the Hearth Fires for generations around various times and tribes.

It was the reason for all the deception, it was the reason for the symbols, it was the reason the big question had gone unanswered.

The answer was simple, yet widely spoken of in the commonalities of religions.

This was the Love, the shimmering heart of the Dragon, the fire of our blood, the reason to be alive.

In order to get this message out, she had needed to do just that, stay alive.

She had to wonder again about the final piece of the puzzle, after finding it.

She must return the story to the People.

How did you do that, when words had been so twisted and mis-used that their very echo caused doubt in the hearts of truth.

She wondered, again, how to begin.

"Words," she thought, "You begin with words."

"What are words but an echo of the feeling within? How does one begin to describe the feeling with-in?" she thought.

Have you ridden on the back of a rattlesnake, or fallen continuously, waiting for the fangs or the ground? Won the lottery again and again, yet to find out each time it was a joke.

For surely nobody who can snuggle up in the dark of heart and rides the wave of human emotion, tumbling along the bottom, could find a path to Love.

Perhaps words were no longer of use.

Rain dreamt deeply.

She woke feeling darkness pushing her down, she could hardly breathe or see.

She fought the urge to gasp for breath and slowed herself down.

She let her eyes adjust and saw stars above.

This helped to bring her back from the abyss threatening to take her away. This dark heavy weight had followed her around always.

If she was not careful, it dragged her to the depths of pain and sor-row, she drowned in.

Listening the call of an owl, then another farther off, begged to be heard.

She let this powerful call of death threatening to soothe her into being present in her body, then and there.

She held onto Dasher, stroking his fur.

The weight lifted and she grate-fully sobbed and fell back into a now dreamless state.

She received a Light bath from her guardian Angels who rocked her and held her while she slept, so she would wake feeling held and sup-ported.

Rain still could not see who she really was, or see these Angels.

She knew they were there.

She was starting to see them, at times, in the right light.

One was her Grandmother. It had only increased her Power, being murdered, but Rain still missed her.

She sighed in her sleep, as the Angels soothed her and did an an-cient healing matrix, undoing the damage done when she had been poisoned.

The illness had not been planned for.

A surprise attack.

The task at hand required com-plete healing on multiple levels for Reagan Bauer to be ready to be who she was meant to be.

There was no time for more sur-prises. The watching increased.

CHAPTER VI

LIGHT WORKERS

"I believe in aristocracy, though if that is the right word, and if a democrat may use it. Not aristocracy of power... but... of the sensitive, the considerate... Its members are to be found in all nations and classes, and through the ages. There is a secret understanding between them when they meet. They represent the true human tradition, the one permanent victory of our queer race over cruelty and chaos. Thousands of them perish in obscurity, a few are great names. They are sensitive to others as well as themselves, they are considerate without being fussy, their pluck is not in swankiness but the power to endure..."

E. M. Forster
The Highly Sensitive Person

Being an extra sensitive human meant she felt her own emotions, deep and dark, and the emotions of those around her.

She recently had begun to be able to separate her own from the surrounding ones.

Feeling the quickening need of the planet to be seen and heard, even in Her dark and hurt.

Much like the internal need to not see the reflection within, people tended, especially in modern days to ignore the darkening cries by distracting themselves, she thought.

She was distracted now.

Thinking was not helping, but she let her mind go there anyway.

Remembering how she had gotten right here took her back lifetimes. Rain needed to stay present in this Heart, but for just a moment she flashed back to treasure hunting with a fellow Rainbow.

This was as the Tribe had prophesied, the ones who took down the walls. Together they had accidentally stumbled into the Carre Shinob Mine.

The forbidden caverns had been blazed into her memory.

The legendary gold mines were being guarded, continuing the cycle of greed and allowing an alien species to farm our planet of our precious resources of Air and Water, while the species here, Humans bickered over a shiny metal, thinking this was the precious resource.

The simple trick had worked for lifetimes, but now that the warriors were awakening, Gaia stood a chance.

She needed to get to the springs so she could relax and focus.

Remembering she needed something else, carefully Rain brought her energy to a slower vibration.

What was she supposed to remember?

She felt so confused and just then a jet flew over spewing a toxic trail. She took out the Organite and directed a healing beam toward the chemicals. They dissipated into radiant green and purple light beams which showered the people around with good feelings instead of toxins.

The jet operator radioed his ship above and told them that he had found Rain, but did not know this was not needed. Her spinning out in time was a clear signal.

They already had her, but were just watching and waiting for the right moment. It had been decided to let the girl live, as she held mysterious power that the Queen was going to need to destroy the last strongholds of magic.

Her strength was surprising to them, and her will to live and fight for her planet, zealous.

They had determined Rain would be useful.

Her race was tired too, and enough humans were awakening and not feeding the drama machines, the battle was heating up.

Shankar ordered more spraying, more horrible news, more chaos, more toxins, more distractions, new devices and games to occupy human minds and keep them sick, fighting and struggling.

Many were giving up.

It had been so easy until now, but then again there had been deception on the human's side, they had hidden answers and weapons of Light all over and the army gathered, ready to take the planet back.

Most of them were unaware of their own roles and importance, and how each choice affected the whole world.

Shankar sat in her high, dark, ornate command center and flicked the screen in front of her to a man beating a woman, a young child watched in horror from the corner as he came to her next.

The Queen inserted the thought he needed to touch, feel and play games with this girl, his granddaughter.

The Queen fueled on the pain and plugged herself into the shadow, inserting guilt, shame and secrecy, continuing the abuse, feeding her race with the dark emotions and pain of the easily influenced minds of these pathetic creatures.

They so easily injured one another.

She cussed a serpent's worst word,

"Love," she screamed!

The Angels came and took the girl's soul to the gentle land where she learned about herself and magic, and how to go to this place inside, when she needed to.

The pain she felt transformed into strength and healing for others.

She had contracted to experience this, and was a great warrior of Light, critical to the fight to set things right.

The little girl huddled in the corner, snuggling her stuffed dog, but a seed had been planted, and she knew deep down, she would be all right, as her Soul was an internal flame of Love, she simply needed to shine it on the dark.

She saw inside her mind, a strange looking creature glaring at her.

The creature saw her See and shrank away, leaving a delightful pink bubble behind her.

The girl fell into a deep sleep, and woke up years later, in a big body, ready to begin.

Warriors were made to remember that in order to win, the dark needed to be felt.

Each contracted to experience abuse and trauma, have many dark challenges, and if they came through, could spread great healing and prepare the bridge between Source and Heart.

These were the Lightworkers.

Rain had been amongst the first of the generation brought in specifically for the challenges ahead.

They had a new aura and were named, Indigos.

They had been in training for lifetimes.

She was to help awaken the truth within these souls that needed it.

CHAPTER VII

FREE WILL PLANET

"Earth is a free will zone and the creator Gods fought over ownership. Entities took over that did not want humans to know the truth. They were easier to control that way. Darkness is a lack of information, Light is information. We have been on a limited broadcast and need to change the channel. There is wealth in the emotions mined by the alien forces. It connects you to your spiritual body allowing you to see with ancient eyes connecting the purpose. Activate your memories as members of the Family of Light, branch renegades, ambassadors. Change the station. Dial into love."

Paraphrased from Pleiadan Message for 2012,
A Wake Up Call

Above, Shankar laughed with the throaty, hissing, mirth of dark intent.

The dark cloud had reached her.

"Yes," thought the Queen, she has forgotten.

Let her go, but only in this fog.

She must forget the cave and stay locked in the visions of her past.

"Back off," she hissed to her guards.

Rain sat outside the line of pictographs now, confused and stuck remembering.

"When was it?"

It all felt very familiar.

"Perfect, now that our kind are there, in the town, ready, disguised?"

"Yes, my Queen," replied Dakoner, the Queen's most trusted servant.

"We have a couple there. They were easy to embody and take over. Both of them had deep emotional wounds and heavy pain bodies. Our blenders have been given permission to use whatever trickery needed to keep her confused and sick."

The blenders were Serpentine who could assume shapes and forms, human included. The body they took over still functioned and held it's own dominion, but was easily influenced by the energy within.

It was a voice that sounded like their own, directing them. Only in certain light and if the blender was shooting controlling waves from the eyes could they be spotted within their human host.

The human had no idea why they reacted to certain things as they did, and just thought they were

going more and more insane, not realizing that it was an entity keeping them from their true selves and controlling thoughts, actions and deeds.

Many humans had been taken over, numerous in high-ranking positions.

It was rumored the President himself was embodied by an alien force.

Humans were in deep trouble.

Rain was returning to many challenging situations, and she desperately needed rest.

Her family had held a high-ranking status amongst the secret societies vowing to protect the magic and hold Gaia until She could be won again. The magic was delicate and needed strengthening and protection.

The protection had to come at all costs.

Even if it meant making sure Rain did not fail, by allowing her to sacrifice herself, in the event she had to. Her failure would mean the failure of the whole planet, so this could not be allowed.

This was why she could not know the weight of it, why they left her alone, why she needed to go through her challenges.

A heavy weight rested on her heart.

In order to bring the Light she had needed to get snuggled up and cozy to her enemy, the Shadow of her self, her irrational and constantly chattering mind had to be still.

She had spent much time training in martial arts, dance, meditations, eastern practices, she had studied with Shamans, soothsayers, great teachers, and spent much time alone.

She constantly strove to be better, as she had a deep longing to change the desperate and dying world.

She felt she had to.

It was her reason to be alive.

Her quest, her mission.

She would succeed or die trying.

She turned up the String Cheese Incident and sang along.

"Gonna pick myself up off the ground, when that feeling comes around. Sometimes it seems like such a hard life, but there's good times around the bend. Roller coaster gotta fall to the bottom to climb to the top again."

Messing up the words, she did not care, she sang loudly.

Letting her mood dissipate to the wind and music she remembered to look at her surroundings.

She palmed the small, burnt red, intricately carved Dragon, and then placed it on the dash.

It was her favorite object so far.

It reminded her of her father and grandmother telling a creation story to her about the Mother Dragon, and the people hiding her in the lake. Her sons and daughters resting in various alpine lakes and below the mountains.

The jewels scattered in the hills are scales and hold great magic, but belong only to Dragon Riders with pure hearts, who use the magic for healing.

The People were all getting along until an unfamiliar species appeared. They were not like "The People" and never were content,

they needed more and more.

They stole magic and wanted great Power.

They spoke untruths, which "The People" did not understand.

A great Council was formed and it was decided that the magic must be hidden and only brought out at the right time, by the right people.

It was sealed.

Only this bloodline could awaken the Dragon, so She would not be in danger.

The bloodline must be hidden and protected too, with the Royal Dragon Riders and Friends, being secreted away in unlikely bodies and places.

The Tribes divided and spread these secrets out, and spread the magic out and around.

Messages and codes were hidden in stones, buried below mountains and in caverns, with only symbols to mark the way.

The waste of the Mother Dragon was gold.

It held great power and magic, but this magic was not in the metal itself, but the ability to awaken the sleeping heart.

When the heart was awake, humans were powerful and radiant.

They were the only ones who carried the ability to transform negative emotions and thoughts into Light.

This was the magic.

The new alien species, having been kicked out of other places in the Universe thought they would just wait, as they wanted this planet and the magic it held.

So, the story was told.

They watched and waited, but

now it was heating up and the time for the big fight had begun.

The aliens had destroyed many of the great protective devices, such as pyramids.

Many had been disguised below mountains and oceans and they just now realize this, as the humans were somehow still holding Gaia.

They needed in, they needed to destroy the rest of the magic lines, the Dragon, Her children and any real humans left. Or they would be forced to find another pathetic little place to trick and steal.

Shankar fumed.

"Maybe they are not so pathetic and puny. This one is hard to get rid of, and I think we need her."

"We will make sure she gets what she needs to help us with our victory."

"In the mean time let's have some fun with this town."

They turned up the chemical sprays, tapped into the unconsciousness and watched the strife begin.

Shankar realized that once the chest was opened, Universal Law would send them back to the void.

CHAPTER VIII

SPIRIT OF ADVENTURE

"Man could escape danger only by renouncing adventure, by abandoning that which has given the human condition its unique character and genius among the rest of living things. The Earth is not a resting place. Man has elected to fight, not necessarily for himself, but for a process of emotional, intellectual and ethical growth that goes on forever. To grow in the midst of dangers is the fate of the human race, because it is the law of the spirit."

William T. Close
The Earth is not a Resting Place

Deeply dreaming and lost in the past, Rain thrashed on the ground of her tipi remembering a particularly dangerous find and trying to find her way in time.

The day began early, the two women set out before dawn to begin the arduous work of removing the chest from its resting place.

Shelby and Rain were a great treasure hunting team.

The day threatened storms and the wind had already begun its furious spiraling, heralding a storm.

Heading to the parking spot just where the blaze was, they set out.

Careful to check for unwanted visitors, with technology these days, you could extract endless data from one thread.

"You see any cars, Shelby?"

"No."

"OK, keep your eyes peeled. This spot is so good, I can hardly stand it."

This was, after all, a treasure worth millions and a huge threat to the powers that kept greed prevailing.

Lugging as little as possible to the spot, the women were cheerful and felt alive.

Shelby had found three hawk feathers and stuck them in her rainbow knit hat.

Her long auburn hair tumbled out and blew across her face.

She sputtered and laughed.

Rain had never seen Shelby upset, and admired her calm outlook.

It was one of the reasons they got along so well, the balance was there.

Rain tended to be quick and hyper and needed the grounding energy. Shelby needed the motivation.

The beauty of mountain air and view of the lake below had her spirits high.

The women chatted and joked about Forrest.

"Betcha Forrest came here all alone. I woulda come with ya. Where's da box, Forrest, you sneak?"

Laughing loudly, they trudged through spiky sagebrush, and followed dry Fenn Creek to where it split.

The crisp cool air had the bite of fall and dew still rested on tender leaves. Scaring a small rabbit, Rain's heart skipped a beat.

She was nervous at this spot.

Though she had not seen them, she felt them.

As she had gotten closer and closer to the location of the chest, she noticed they were more and more careful to stay far enough out of site to not be seen, yet did not care she noticed.

Or did not know.

Catching the tiny glint of looking glass, in the far distance, they had not evaded them this time.

"Look over there."

"Where?" Shelby craned.

"Right down there, see the glass shining? "

"Oh, yeah, crap."

"It's OK, if the box is in here, we can get it out without them seeing, we will distract them, like this." Rain mooned the looker.

Shelby and Rain cackled and kept digging.

The location was too good to just pass up.

They dug until nightfall and the hole itself began to collapse.

Until this time, they had discussed that, indeed, Forrest would have put it this deep.

"Gosh, he does like digging, right?"

"Why don't we have a metal detector?"

"Well, he would bury it below three feet, but in here we could at least check."

"Couple of hippy girls, have no idea how to be treasure hunters," Shelby giggled, as rocks tumbled into their hole.

Looking out, Rain sighed and thought to herself this would be the perfect grave.

Forrest intended to put his bones with the chest.

A person would never be found in a thousand years.

Just what Forrest had wanted.

She had a moment of self-pity.

If she did not feel better soon, she would come to this spot to kill herself. She would not wind up plugged into machines.

Alas, they had not struck bronze as intended, but a small box, containing a glowing purple stone, radiant with iridescent light when held right.

The colors blended into a smoothly cold and delicious grape sherbet, melting in the winter sun.

She thought it looked tasty.

Shelby pulled out a snack.

"Hey, girl, you are so on top of it!"

Rain and Shelby looked at the stone some more then put it in Rain's lumpy leather amulet pouch.

The stone had been embedded with part of a song key code, it happily chimed several notes when placed in the pouch.

The frustration of being one step behind the Chroma was beginning to get to her. She struggled to be happy with finding just the stone.

"Look out," screeched Shelby as a loud sound screamed by her head.

Her daydreaming had almost caused that second they had been waiting for.

The powers that be must also think she was close to actually fire on them with obvious lethal intent.

Rain's heart hammered and for a second, she froze.

Her martial arts kicked in, finally, and she rolled and then sprang to a crouch, she grabbed Shelby's arm and pulled her along a zigzag run to shelter.

When the reached the edge of the woods, panting and wheezing, relief flooded through her. She knew it would not last as they were still coming and she had used most of the energy reserves while digging.

They pushed on, straining for the energy to keep going.

She realized they had nearly caught up and a piece of flying bark lodged a way into her arm.

They needed to find something and find it fast.

Thinking she might collapse, instead Rain thought of her mission and willed her self to keep going.

They clumsily dashed across a clear stream and a past existence shoved itself into her being.

She held the gash in her arm tightly as she ran.

A blood trail was no good.

It stopped bleeding. She noticed that it was not deep.

She would look later.

She knew she had been here before, the place felt chillingly familiar and forbidden, but they had to keep going.

Scrambling along a ledge, Rain's eye caught a signature scratched in the stone.

She barely could process that she was seeing "Butch Cassidy" scrawled on the under side of this ledge.

Moving so fast, her heart hammered against her chest, she would look at that later.

Shelby pressed on, but Rain could tell, she also was tiring.

They inched their way upward on a series of ledges that did not appear to hold a way up, but as they were there, the women found an old trail of sorts.

There were interesting markings and less than obvious foot placement.

They had blindly leaped out to the rocks as a way to throw the tracking and had gotten lucky.

They inched their way upward.

Near the top, covered by a large boulder, was a crack that looked dark from where they crawled up.

Rain knew that the chill down her spine meant she needed to pay attention.

They poked their heads into the musty smelling crevasse on the ledges.

It did not smell of animal, but held the crackling snap of Power.

Taking a quick second to ask the Earth's permission for refuge, the quick flash of light leading in was a welcome sign.

They carefully, slowly and reverently entered.

It took a second for their eyes to adjust, but it slowly began to dawn on Rain they were sitting in one of the protected caves of Aztec treasure.

She gaped.

The Ute Indians, ancestors, descendants of the Aztecs had kept greedy hands from coming near.

Threats of death, imminent and slow, were enough to keep the most hearty of treasure hunters out of the Carre Shinob.

Now the women were sitting in the mine full of secrets and answers.

Looking around at the various tunnels, they picked the one with the giant Sun and moved down the golden hallway, to a room with pillars of solid gold, a throne and giant disks with intricate patterns. Walls were adorned with hieroglyphs and Rain noticed a picture carved.

It was of a Dragon, cave and a lake, reminding her of the stories from childhood.

There was a long, dark haired woman in a flowing white robe, wearing an intricate amulet with a golden claw hanging from it.

It was surrounded by animal fetishes.

Was that the necklace in the box?

Time seemed to bend and the wind blew through her hair.

She felt a chilling recognition of the whole story carved into the golden walls.

The chest was towards the end of the story line that came back around and ended where it began.

Mirroring itself across the room, the opposite seemed to reflect.

Showing both sides simultaneously, transcending time. The brain was not seeing it, but her heart felt the truth in the pictures.

Showing a group of hundreds of light skinned people living in caverns peacefully, the story showed them coming from Atlantis, living in what is now North America before the Spanish Invasion.

The secrets of the alchemy of the gold, dragons, pyramids and stories of the Ancients lay told here and why to cover the truth of it.

Keys to unlocking the doors were written.

Pictures of huge alien ships with horrible creatures above Gaia, mining the intent and energy inside the magic metal.

Rain felt the chill as the walls wrapped around.

She did not go farther down the corridor to see it continue wrapping back around in time.

The Wheel carved as time ran around a circle, the end was not there yet. Halting where they stood, marveling, they were sure someone had seen, not the men trying to kill them.

It would only be a matter of time before the Guardian came to them, if they stayed in the cavern.

She knew Butch, her recent hero, and also relative, had been allowed refuge for months at a time here and that he would sooner cut off his own finger than take even the smallest piece.

Rain agreed, and said to Shelby, "If you value your life at all, ever, the last bit of this stays here and you forget how we got to it. There is a bunch of controversy and tons of curses on this. The answers in here are important to us, so look around, take only with your eyes."

They feasted.

Shelby nodded with her mouth agape, turning in slow circles, tears streaming down her face.

A few ledges down, a man radioed his boss.

"They got away, I cannot see where they disappeared to."

"It looks like she found something again."

"Damn that girl, this is my box."

"We will catch her next time. Go to her car and see what you find, then just get back."

"OK, over and out."

The dark haired man said to the radio.

He puzzled over the rich man looking for the treasure and why he would be so interested in the tall skinny girl.

It seemed he had enough money, and was just playing a game.

He never revealed his identity to the sharpshooter, just gave lots of cash, directions to watch, follow, scare, not kill, report it all back.

The man was particularly interested in pictures from camp life and any activities.

He wanted to know everything about the young girl.

There were a couple others he was paid to follow and watch as well.

This one kept him busy and seemed to sense him there.

She usually looked directly at his looking glass.

He was beginning to respect this girl and what she was going through, coming out, looking mighty fine, he daydreamed, as he headed back to where his dark and decked out SUV was.

The eccentric man paid for all of it.

He settled in to wait for the girls to resurface.

He was enjoying this game immensely and the pile of cash was much needed.

He might just grab the treasure when this girl found it.

Anyone could look for it.

Who said he could not cheat?

Rain was the closest and had found a bunch of little objects she hoarded in the ugly old pouch around her neck.

She only took it off to sleep, the black and white dog she had would keep him out.

Dasher had come to his hiding spot once and scared the man so badly, he had just about messed himself.

Rain and Shelby had been setting up their camp, laughing and were changing.

Just as he was focusing his looking glasses better, he felt the eyes.

He had to look for a while, but then the dog was suddenly right there.

He raised his lips in a low growl, crouched, sprang, landed right in front of the looking glass, spilling the green thermos of coffee, and scaring him so much, he shook for hours.

That had been the night before.

He had been careful to be downwind, but as much as Rain knew he was there, that big dog surely did.

He was glad the dog stuck by her side, closely.

It helped his plans.

He could play games really well, he thought.

He had been trained to just wait patiently for as long as it took, this game was enjoyable, especially the women.

He did not care too much for the searcher called Tully.

He kept his search very public, so was easy to track, and usually pretty far off the actual places.

He was too caught up in the glory and missed the basics of the poem.

Forrest Fenn did not want the finding of the chest public.

It would ruin his plan.

Forrest had not thought anyone would actually get close to it, and protected the articles within.

Tully would not be allowed to get it, even if he figured out the location, which he had, but missed the rest of the meaning.

He had stood five hundred feet from the resting place.

He had stood there with Forrest.

Getting through Forrest was the last clue.

He enjoyed the publicity and friendship, so just watched from his home as the players gamed, and felt a touch sorry for Tully.

The cute girls were more interesting and enjoyable to him.

The one who called herself, Rain, had found his small treasures, which irritated, but was intriguing to him.

He collected unusual objects, powerful items.

Rain fascinated him.

He felt a strange connection to her.

She reminded him of a younger self.

He also worried for her.

He knew she was sick, and infected with finding the chest.

If anyone was to win, he rooted for her.

She might just do the right thing with his important charge, the Chroma.

He preferred the objects stay hidden, they were safer.

His puzzle was supposed to be unsolvable.

Why was this one solving it?

He fidgeted at his antique desk and waited for the reports, fantasizing about dominating her with soft sincerity and promises of support, he knew she needed.

She had contacted him several times, and had even left him a gift.

He made her wait, but did tell her he would meet her.

CHAPTER IX

ANCIENT ALCHEMY

"The Utes are not simply protecting a treasure: they are protecting their sacred heritage and preserving their history and identity as a people... Carre-Shinob is their last stronghold against white encroachment... treasure hunters are a relentless breed... Search if you must, and best of luck to you. I have seen what you will never find and it is fabulous!"

Kerry Ross Boren
The Gold of Carre-Shinob

They needed to stay either way.

Rain supposed she would rather face the Guardian than the sharp shooter aiming at them.

The stories whispered also spoke of those who never made it out of this area, when searching for this mine.

The oath to protect it had been passed down from generation to generation in the Ute tribe.

There was a rumor that this mine was felt to be owned by the Mormon Church, and that the prophecies of their church spoke of LDS members as being the only ones with gold to back the debt once the system collapsed.

The Mormon Church claims it was prophesied by the natives, the secret was to go to Brigham Young.

Conspiracy trickery and falsification of documentation changed history and the possible future.

Great catastrophe would reign if the rest of the secrets were given over to corrupt church members.

Greed, abuse and general frustration in the church was so high, Rain hoped the leaders of the Ute nation, her relatives, would never willingly hand over the gold to a religious institution that lied, murdered, kidnapped and stole to arrive in the present.

The true teachings were of course, beautiful, laying in the Chroma, protected from time.

The women felt the chill of evening blow into the cavern, felt pretty safe to assume they had been missed by the very least, the one shooting at them.

As Shelby snored, Rain drifted into a deep sleep.

She let her eyes rest on a beautiful Gold Dragon, flying above a lake.

She dreamt of one of the places she traveled in her dreams.

She was always running and looking for someone or something.

These dreams must have a deep meaning, as she returned there again and again.

This mine was sacred to her people, but it was not what she sought.

There must be ties and gold from the Seven Cities of Cibola, in the chest.

Her life was unfolding into a pattern beyond her control, and

these caverns had something to do with it.

The Guardian knew they were there, knew the intent was to not touch, take or tell, so let it go, but watched.

He had reason to keep Rain safe.

She was family, but did not know his identity.

This was how the secrets got passed along and kept out of the wrong greedy hands.

Only one knew the secrets, carried generationally, and held the highest honor without acknowledgement, except for burial rights in the caverns.

Protecting this last cache and the secrets within at all cost.

Rain was part of the secret.

Her family held high-ranking status in the general secret Tribal Council that had been formed generations ago.

It had been formed when the first invaders came.

This Council was deeply linked to the energetic and Universal Council watching her.

The Council was built on the idea of unity and peace amongst the planet would come through the threads of commonalities and love, which had to be nourished.

The challenges ahead were foreseen, and to protect the simple truth, it had been hidden, only to be seen through the veil of self.

Seeing through the layers of dark and pain came first.

CHAPTER X

DREAMS ARE BORN IN THE FUTURE

"There can be no doubt about the existence of the
mines, not the least are several maps and consider-
able ore in possession of the (Mormon). Don't bother
to ask... Their policy is to deny any knowledge of it...
before the church policy changed and forbade access.
I have seen enough to be assured of the Churches
knowledge of the existence of the mines... They
exists in the Church's documents... It is the repository
of Montezuma's vast treasure, the same loss Cortez
lamented. There can be no doubt that the sacred relics
of the Aztecs-ancestors of the Utes were returned to the
source from which the gold came. There is not a more
sacred site among the Native American people than
Carre-Shinob."

Kerry Ross Boren
The Gold of Carre-Shinob

Running down a dark hall of a building half way in ruins, Reagan felt sweat run down her legs and roll into her eyes, blinding her for a minute.

She tried to remember the way.

It was down this corridor, just outside the elevator doors, if she ran, up to the next floor, she knew there was a room she could get into.

On this side of the building, everything was normal.

It was a fancy hotel, complete with fountains, thick green and gold carpet, and gold inlay on all the fixtures.

She panted and heaved the door open, running now, in thick carpet that seemed to pull her into it.

Sweaty fear blinded her.

She reached the door and gently pushed into the room.

They had just been here; the bathroom was still steaming with scented air. Though there was a stillness and a quiet that invaded into her, a deep lonely knowledge, they ran ahead again.

Her dreams allowed her to go to this place and to have an ability to navigate, though it was a strange land.

There were places she flew to again and again.

Rain could map it here.

The huge river flowed into a sea, and the city rested at the edge.

The future was where she was visiting.

A potential future.

It was the one they were all running from.

What she did understand was that she searched for something, knew her way around, was seemingly invisible, traveled to the same destinations.

Some of the destinations held danger, others, people she needed to see, but could only find the remnants of them, saw their pictures on the small refrigerator, caught the steam from the shower, but not yet the people themselves.

She kept running. In this section, there were brutal guards with big guns who were hunting her type.

Those who had refused to be implanted, not taking the immunizations they pushed, eventually being rounded up into camps, the dissidents were slowly disappearing.

It was too late though. Many citizens of Gaia had unknowingly allowed themselves to be injected with nano-particles, meant to be the first tracking devices with internal brain control.

Disguised as vaccines for the masses for the great outbreak sensationalized by the press.

Also with the new drones, they were able to get those who refused, only a few were left alive and not imprisoned.

Since then, these few have been hunted.

They are the only ones the ill intending dark forces could not control. Victory would have been quietly won by the dark, whilst the infected worked at will for the alien forces of darkness, the Serpentine Race, the Sagiditis.

People so easily controlled by the devices the World depended on.

Cell phones, pagers, TV's, microwaves, massive satellites circled and could pin point locations and emit frequencies to disrupt regular brain wave patterns.

Rain ran harder than she had before and the slow drag of the dream pulled her to a heavy panicked thickness.

They gained ground, she ran, bumping into a wall, nearing the end of the long corridor, just around the corner, was another safe spot.

This spot offered a car that took her through forested land by the coast. Where there was warm clear water, she often went out to Sea.

A crackling, snapping noise jostled her awake.

It took a second after traveling to this land to come back.

There it was, the sound that had awoken her.

She stilled her breath and listened with her whole being to the sound.

Straining her ears, the soft crunch of leaves and the subtle snap of twigs, something slowly headed their way.

Just gaining full consciousness, hearing the movement getting closer to the entrance of the cave, Rain held her breath.

Shelby's breathing indicated she had not been awakened by the sound.

Time slowed and her breath began to ache.

She heard a quick snort and rustle and realized, whatever it was had left when it smelled them.

As her heart hammered back to a normal beat, Rain stilled her mind and started a morning stretching routine she had been doing for years.

She drew the power into her with her breath and intention and felt her mind loosen as her muscles awoke.

"A way opens before us, all obstacles are released, energy comes up from the great Center, then makes a circle, bathing you, bathing me, bathing Her in Light."

She turned in each direction and honored the Sun as her ancestors did every morning.

CHAPTER XI

DIMENSIONALLY STUCK

"I am very old. I have seen many things, but I am Indian and
cannot say much... To my people the mines are sacred. The
gold belongs to my people. I know where there is enough
gold to buy all the things in the white man's world. But
Happy Jack is Indian and will not tell it. I am Happy Jack
and I am rich, for Towats believes me."

From Happy Jack's Journal in
The Gold of Carre-Shinob

The bigger problem of getting out of the hills loomed.

She knew the man, whoever they represented, was patient and would be waiting for her to resurface.

When it was time to return to the present, she wondered, again, what were the lessons in those words and memories associated with it?

She remembered the distraction picked up as the vibration of the Heart resonated.

Was this what was happening to her?

Was she stuck in another dimension of past memory?

How that could hold onto you and swallow you.

That must be the answer.

She exhaled the simplicity and again got to the task at hand, reaching the sacred Springs.

The dawn was snapping crisp fingers to a fall morning.

Rain realized she had been dreaming again in the realm of the past and had let time slide past her.

The world was at a critical point and she could not allow her mind to wander into these dream realms.

With focused intent, she gathered herself to journey onward.

Dusting herself off, she wondered how long she had fallen asleep?

This felt familiar.

She took a lingering look at the Flathead River, smooth and green, running with a determined current. She decided to press on to town.

It had been years since she had been home.

The road twisted and turned and rolled over to the flat section that stretched into the old lake's washout zone.

She loved this country and the desolate quietness it offered.

People minded their business on the reservation, but it did not mean gossip was not hot.

She was tickled at the stir she was about to create and blasted the music louder.

A couple hawks soared, searching for prey, and then Rain felt the vortex of the area, she saw the edge of it as she drove through and had to chuckle as the clock in her VW stopped.

She loved this timeless place.

The painful memories, reminders of her childhood, running free on the Reservation, being educated about her People, by her Grandparents and her Dad.

He was a distant man and had married into a rich white family, shaming his Native one.

The prejudices reached all around.

He had gone to Vietnam and not come back the same, but had found a love for surgery, which he eventually pursued.

He packed up his family, except Rain, who they left in Montana, at Spring Creek, moved east, to study his passion.

Her family still owned land and were very much a part of the Council.

Rain did not know they maintained status.

She felt abandoned by them and still could see her Dad turn his head away from her and not look back.

He had hardly spoken to her; Rain felt she deeply disappointed him.

Her fondest and last memories of any time spent with him, he had been telling her the same creation story as grandmother, with Dragons and Rainbow bridges, Twins, a magic chest and an Indian Princess from long ago, who can awaken the Old Magic within the People.

She felt a lonely pang, but quickly let it pass.

She waved at the familiar looking cop and drove into town.

CHAPTER XII

TWINS

When I am worried about my condition
I vow with all beings
to rest in my human condition:
breathing in, breathing out, heart beat.

Robert Aitken
*The Dragon Who Never Sleeps: Verses for
Zen Buddhist Practice*

After dropping her things, she pulled in front of the Symes Hotel and scanned the lot for his jeep, but she knew he was in New Mexico and married.

It had been destined when they had met years before.

The spark between them had raged within her for all of this time, past and present, he filled her dreams.

She dreamed of his piercing eyes and contagious laugh, of being in his arms throughout time.

Sighing and swallowing the swell threatening to overrun her lids, Rain got out and took a long look around.

She thought she was past longing for him, the sights and smells brought the feelings rushing in.

The dusty beige dilapidated buildings had not changed much and were falling apart.

This was a relief in the world that shifted into fanciness.

The neon sign flashed Symes, dogs ran in the lot, chasing one another.

Dasher got out and smelled the wagon wheel where many messages were left by canine pals and not.

"Dasher is in town, don't mess with my gal, I will rip ya to shreds, and if there are any hot ladies who wanna look at deer, I am out by the Pyramid Mountain. Later."

He let a long stream out and looked lovingly at Rain.

He watched her carefully to see what this place meant besides a social hour. It seemed to be a good place, but he did smell his enemy.

He sniffed around, keeping one wary eye on her; no serpent scum was getting close to her. What he could not help was the influence of the blenders.

A brunette, older, walked by, wearing a too tight bright blue string bikini. She talked loudly in a high-pitched tone.

He growled lowly, inaudible to humans, this one heard and glared at him, but was quick to turn her smile back on as she and the blonde man she was with hopped into the Springs.

They were here already.

He would be busy.

Rain felt safe.

She was distracted though.

She did not sense the danger in the pools as she allowed the water to soak in.

She chit-chatted with the two.

It turned out they too were from Salt Lake, recently.

Rain had a nagging feeling, but ignored it.

She drifted off for a while and listened to the woman talking with her partner.

Rain had run over her cell last week.

She, after all, had to be careful.

It was so easy to be traced.

She was not aware how many followed or why they needed to find her.

She thought again how wrong she had been to trust that her location was secret, as long as she had the first trackers for humans, a cell phone, they could find her.

Rain made the one call, to her Mom, in Wyoming.

She had been asleep when the quiet cracklings had begun.

The forces of the darkness popping against her barriers set up, her guardian dog, Dasher, growling fiercely.

Taxing to send them flying back, with her shield.

She had used a strong Jadeite crystal.

It had worked, but exploded.

A black SUV had tried following her the next day, too.

She ditched them, she thought.

Rain felt good that this place had remained a stronghold against the advances of time that had caused so many to lose their own abilities and to be easily controlled, located and eliminated.

The urgency to rest in the magic of the Springs called her.

She was feeling sick.

Her head pounded, sharp pains reminded her to take her medicine.

The Springs would help.

She sighed as she eased into the hottest pool.

She closed her eyes and drifted.

This was not her first trip into the heart of the Dragon, having been there, lifetimes ago.

Recently she had begun to see how the patterns in her life had been set, so she could see this past.

A nagging idea and twisting fear rose at the thought of the urgency and the need to find something.

She had been told, by the objects, to come to this place.

She simply had to open and let go enough to see clearly.

Study more.

Shaking the demons off her back and waking to the quest, had been set in motion before she had returned in this body, on this plane of time on the planet called, Gaia.

Her mission was a simple one, but as it held the key to unlocking the hearts of many warriors of the Light, it had been hard to get to exactly where she was right now.

Close to the Heart.

Rain heard him before she saw him.

She would know that laugh anywhere.

It reached the roots of her soul with sparks of intense heat.

"Why was he here?"

That was why the feeling was so strong.

She grew flushed and started shaking, hoping he had not felt her yet.

Just as this thought occurred, he turned, slowly, meeting her eyes, and in it she saw the same confusion mirrored.

Here was a soul mate, their passion having long ago been shelved and boxed up tightly.

He was married and she had a mission.

This must be an illusion Rain reasoned, but when he walked towards her, all hopes of the illusion vanished with her choked exhalation.

"Hey there."

"Hey, hey."

It felt hotter outside, Rain flushed.

"I thought you were in New Mexico?"

After all of these years, and after all of the other attempts to forget and move on, how could she when this man rocked her to her depths and she knew this was the one they talk about.

She flashed on the image of him holding the remains of their two-month-old baby to bury and the rip never repaired, and knew this must be a final key in the puzzle.

Her heart had not healed and perhaps they must join again and heal to ignite the flame in the heart of the Dragon.

What of his wife, she guiltily remembered.

Rain's pulse beat chaotic rhythms against her head; her heart fired out the emerald green rays of the twin flame and felt his spark as well.

It was a pull neither could resist.

Behind him, she saw the small woman approaching.

Intense in her stride.

In the same instance, Rain expanded so; she contracted again and pulled herself inward, realizing she had crossed a boundary.

Shamed, she flushed and burned as they both now approached.

She stammered out a forced, "Nice to meet you."

When the introductions had been made.

Kieran left out their history.

Rain was a friend.

Though she could feel the woman's confusion, saw the puzzled glance.

He had not told his wife, Sarah.

Preparing for an awkward moment, Rain steeled against the desire to grab Kieran and smell the wooly scent of his tightly curled locks, let herself drift into two eyes that mirrored hers.

She got through the polite discussions.

Jumping out of the pools, Rain made it just around the corner before the hot tears had fallen.

Sinking into the past, she let several memories flash.

It could not be a coincidence that they had planned a holiday right then.

She knew he had to be a part of the mystery, puzzle and the solution.

What those answers were, Rain decided she would come to later.

Right now she needed to get in touch with the Council, but would have to be patient.

Rain was aware they watched her movement and would come to her if and when they deemed ready, she felt urgent.

She was here now, as promised several lifetimes ago.

The dreams and memories bringing her to the present.

The ship watched in delight as the drama and emotions heightened.

CHAPTER XIII

YOUNG LOVE

"Sometimes music cannot substitute for tears."

Paul Simon

"Oh God," Rain thought.

How the hell am I supposed to just wait, when I can't even wait until morning to let my thoughts collide?

The doubt and fear returned.

"I just don't think I really am the one for this."

Shivering in the midnight air, Rain ran until her blood warmed up.

Then it began to boil, "Why did she have to do this?" she thought with rising panic.

Did the weight really rest on her, like it felt?

She had so many questions and knew as long as those remained, answers would not appear.

Feeling her resentment rising, she pushed harder and let her thoughts slow down a minute.

Across town, another had thoughts.

Sarah wondered how she could have been so blind.

She always knew her husband had been hiding something from his past. His eyes always turned a funny color when he spoke of a certain time, an unnatural turquoise and the sadness resonating from his usually cheerful demeanor was unmistakably tragic and secret.

She had asked him once, "Was there a woman then, in your life?"

To which he had icily replied, "No."

Sarah knew now, the tall and mysteriously beautiful woman they had seen earlier, was the reason for the ice.

Her eyes had been the same color, the otherworldly turquoise, for just an instant. There had been a moment that seemed frozen to her.

As Sarah walked up to her husband and asked, "This woman, was it Rain?

"What kind of a name is Rain?"

"And who was she?"

The energy between Kieran, her husband of several years, and Rain had literally snapped the air and the fire between their eyes was unmistakably hot and alive. Sarah moaned and rolled over; she felt her husband's back and began to rub gently.

The response was not the usual arousal, but an irritated wall surrounded him.

Sarah hurried out of bed before she let him know she was crying, Kieran was not one to be supportive of emotions and held firm to the "no sniveling" philosophy.

Though she knew it was armor only, Sarah was feeling tender enough to feel like escaping outside for a minute.

She stepped onto the balcony, just in time to see Rain run by.

What on Earth is that woman doing running at this hour?

It was then it hit her.

She sat, immediately, onto the chilled stone of the balcony.

The echoes of pounding feet exploded in her head and thundered, as each step grew further her dread grew.

She had already lost him to this woman, Rain, before she had even met him. This was his past he was hiding, and it was much worse than she had thought.

The smell of the Springs below helped her haul herself up.

She knew then what she needed to do.

She was going to go talk to Rain and find out exactly what was missing from the story.

Sarah was a feisty woman, short, with a passion for finding truth.

Her green eyes, short dark hair and classically pretty face were matched with determination and street smarts.

Nobody was going to separate her from the love of her life.

She had met him in Missoula, Montana, a town where possibility collides with intention and the vortex of time wraps you up in sweet mystery.

They had met and fallen in love and pretty quickly had married.

There were things about him she did not know, this was one of them.

"What are you doing out here?" he said stumbling onto the balcony.

"Just checking out the sky," she lied, but then that is what they were doing, right? Lying?

Sarah intended to find out the truth.

In the mean time, she snuggled up to the back of her husband and could feel his internal struggle.

He softened and turned to her, kissing her doubts away.

As Sarah drifted, Kieran guiltily pushed the thoughts of Rain out and turned towards his beautiful wife, holding her gently.

Drifting, he found himself running towards her, trying to grab her flowing robe as she disappeared, yet again, down another corridor, dank with dark smoke from the torches.

Footsteps behind him and he made a turn into a room, barely missing being run over by the mob chasing her.

He had not saved her, again.

Kieran rolled and grumbled in his sleep, across town, Rain did the same. The run had helped her to be able to sleep.

She was in the dream from Egypt, the one where the mob chases her. There he was, they were dreaming together.

It had been a long time since they shared this power.

"How can I focus with them here?"

Rain gulped back the threatening sob and reasoned the burning jealousy away.

She was so close, this was one of the issues that had held her back and had burned a layer of ice firmly around her inner heart.

This man was the only one who had touched that place.

The story they shared together had hurt her so deeply, she remembered knowing that universes heard the shatter when their love broke the barriers of time and again when it had been refused.

The grief they had shared together had been too much.

It was not a matter of stopping loving him; it was a matter of being able to live without him.

Her twin flame.

She wondered if the mission could be completed and felt the possibility of failure sink deeply into her soul and ricochet outward in waves of stormy darkness.

The swirling emotions were just the past, the enemy of Gaia needed to get a hold of the present.

She let her breath even out and thought of the stories of the Dragon lying asleep in the mountains of Montana.

The mother of all of the Dragons was told to be waiting here, for the right time.

She let her imagination take her to the den and whispered a sacred "Namaste," in an ancient language, understood, at their heart level, by all living beings.

She had been taught to hear these sounds.

These ancient notes of energy transformed into words the mind can grasp.

The language was one of the first barriers to unify the planet.

Along with the many ways that had been devised to divide, which let them destroy Gaia, while her citizens sleepwalked.

Her grandmother had taught her these legends and languages.

Rain recently began to understand the legends were truth.

Whenever she had been extremely upset, her grandmother

taught her to fly and dream to these lands.

Here she would be safe.

Here she was home.

Though her emotions roiled, she began to feel the stillness she needed to see.

Her vision always clouded when emotions rolled over them.

Her thought patterns would turn negative and the environment around her would quickly reflect this.

Her training had not been complete.

There was a reason he was here, perhaps to help her let go, but now she could not worry about it.

She and the huge black and white dog, Dasher headed back to her land.

Her heart jumped at the sight of the patrol car parked there.

He stepped out, looking older, but had the same sneer she remembered.

He looked her over too carefully and said,

"Just checking on things, nobody has been out here in awhile."

"Well, Jim, is it? I am great, and you, your wife?"

"We are all good, glad you are back."

He flushed and got in his rig.

She had to remind him of his wife, who had gotten larger with each child, and meaner too.

He waited until she was out of sight then stroked himself angrily, and sped off looking like he had an important task.

Rain had seen the erection and remembered how he had left the flashlight on her too long and looked past the needed time to bust her.

He had had the same perverted look then.

Well, some things do not change much.

If he came back, she would be ready.

She doubted he would though, she was not the same young girl.

CHAPTER XIV

ALIENS

"Carre-Shinob was an Aztec Temple containing the treasure of Montezuma... Fate is often devoid of reason... There can be no doubt that the sacred relics of the Aztecs-ancestors to the Utes were returned from which the gold came from... Mine was a blood oath, and it would be worth my life to violate it. There is no treasure so valuable as to be worth more than life itself... I will say only that I felt a need to make such a record, to honor the memory of those long forgotten, and to clarify once and for all time the question of ownership... It is the sacred treasure of the Utes, and to them only does it belong."

The Gold of Carre-Shinob

Deep in the ship hovering above Gaia, the serpent queen hissed instructions.

"We are so close to taking very last bit of filthy air, horrible water and hearts of the humans."

"Did you not place the disease in her?"

"Yes," stammered the servant of the serpent.

"Why is she awake?" screamed the Queen?

"The Truth Bringer must not be allowed to know her complete role that she is remembering."

"Hurry, and get to that town. Place yourselves to befriend and interfere."

The queen had another plan.

Rain, one of the Atlantean Planetary Task force leaders, had a weakness, Kieran.

She made sure he heard about the chest.

Looking down on Rain's pain, she could see this plan was good, but not working, Rain was letting go. How could she, with the invisible chains tying her to him?

They had made a secret pact, in the halls of Egypt, Rain and Kieran, to come together then be apart.

They had to, to be able to win.

It was beginning to dawn on the serpent queen that perhaps there was stronger magic here than she realized.

She had not been able to exterminate all of the Task Force, just most of them.

The queen slithered off angrily, wondering how she could explain losing this pathetic little planet.

It was not even habitable for them; she never understood the draw to the homely blue place that had a toxic environment for her species.

This was why they aimed to destroy the water and air; they needed a barren place, devoid of oxygen and aimed to steal this planet out from under the inhabitants.

The species, human, was easy to manipulate, with their tender feelings, sensitive systems and a propensity to destroy one another with toxic emotions.

The toxic feelings were fuel for the serpents, the divisions and labels carefully placed, the system built to enslave and steal.

Fear was the best fuel.

"Turn up the chaos, spread bad news, play on the End."

The funny part for the queen was they had no use for the gold and silver they had the humans fighting over.

They just wanted the alchemy of it, which had nothing to do with the metal itself, but with the intent behind it.

"Gold fever" the disease of the serpent, spread across the globe hungering and consuming in its own bloated path. The gold was the ticket to the serpents finally taking a hold of this pocket of the universe.

A living and breathing planet, Gaia, so beautiful and abundant, rich in Love and community, was a target for the hungry serpents that chewed up, spit out and regurgitated planets.

They were the scum of the Universe, the dark outlaw gang, they had fooled the humans and were close to taking it all, taking it as a gift given, as that was what each person chose to do, give it away, by not seeing.

This was the only way it could be taken.

The one rule that even the Serpentine race, Iluminastisis Sagiditis followed, a planet could only be given.

The part that the Universal Task Force left room with, was there was no preventing tricking the population into giving it away.

Greed was planted, the disease took a hold, and in only several hundred years, the planet was on the brink of gifting itself away.

The only hope lay resting within the warriors of Light, within their hearts, waiting to be awakened and used.

Sleeping potions and chips had been carefully placed and hidden, lifetimes of planning and hiding, torture and abuse had befallen the warriors.

The path clearly put before them was choice, and only in a decision to come into Power, could they.

Others in the Universe wondered if they would be successful, and patiently watched and sent what energy and help they could.

The drama unfolding on Gaia was entertainment for dark forces and a deep rift began to form in the Task Force as they watched Rain struggle.

It was not the first time she would have failed them.

She had been tricked and forced to contract and watch the destruction, without being able to help.

She had been able to hide information she would need later and had managed to disguise her true role well, until now.

The great city of Atlantis and all of the magic within lay hidden below the mountains, Rain had asked them to hide it and let her have a chance again, now.

She had blocked all of her memories, placed a chip within, suppressed her Power and chose a painful path.

To be able to see the shadow and pain, she needed to be deeply in it.

She could see now how this fed her enemy, her mind, and how she could stop fueling the beast.

Fog rolled in, blanketing the sleepy town of Hot Springs.

Across the meadow from her tipi, Taz, the local horse celebrity, snorted and pawed at the half frozen ground.

Something was in the air. Taz, belonging to Rattlesnake, a toughened Rainbow, always could sense the changes in the wind.

Taz could be found wandering around the pastures, as much a part of the population as Lucy, the 96-year-old Southerner, a hater of anyone not white.

Lucy had a nasty reputation for sticking anti freeze in cat food, but still was a part of the town.

Taz, on the other hand was a local hero, his picture adorned many magazines.

It was not unknown to see Taz and Rattlesnake riding or driving down Main Street. Rattlesnake would ride in the car, holding the reins as Taz trotted alongside. It was a site to see.

Taz was getting more and more agitated.

She called to him in her mind, and heard his answer in the ancient language.

"Young girl, something is afoot, wrong, the wind is smelling foul with a magic I am not familiar with, be wary, be wary, look out."

"I thank you, honored one."

Animals could be trusted. The voices heard with clear hearts.

Having friends watching was helpful, as the trickery was increasing, the emotions higher, the divisions growing stronger.

The last ditch effort of the Serpent queen would not be a surprise, nor easy.

Keeping this in mind, Rain hopped on her bike for the short ride to town.

She needed to find Rattlesnake and talk to him about Taz.

Rain worried that, with his magic so visible, Taz was a target.

They needed to cloak him and do it before whatever surprise the enemy had in mind arrived.

Time was short. She peddled furiously, begging Taz to go and hide by the Water, until they could reach him.

Rain threw an energy bubble around herself, Taz, Rattlesnake, then the town itself.

She announced her arrival to the wind, so he would hear her approach.

Rattlesnake was under his jeep, dusty legs sticking out, tools scattered and unhappy sounds flew from under.

"Snake."

When he looked up, she knew he had heard.

She gestured silence and nodded her head to the Water.

"Taz."

This was all that was needed.

He sprang as fast as his overworked legs could humanly move; they quickly walked, in silence, to the hiding place.

The source of the ancient Spring was here.

This vortex swirled between worlds and allowed a cloaking in between time and space.

It rested just below the mountain known to ancients as the Dragon's Head, one of the energy centers carefully and secretly maintained.

Here Taz was, waiting.

Taz cried a greeting to Snake and began to hurriedly describe what he was seeing.

He had managed to remote view the snake ship and to see the queen planning.

She had felt him though, and traced him to here.

Though she knew he was right there, he had vanished.

A curse flew and she retreated inward, ready now that she knew just where he was, and one who was able to see her.

Fittingly, the queen hissed to herself, "I will get them all at once."

She had waited for hundreds years for this particular victory.

"I need to hurry and find the chest."

"These bits and pieces have gotten me here. I need to get in that cavern, which is where the chest is, I think."

"I have been dreaming of an old necklace, I think belonged to me. It must be near here."

"It is one of the tuning necklaces hidden. This one opens the cavern, when combined with the Old Dance."

"If Taz thinks you are in danger, Sister, then be careful, he is really babbling about weird things, and is pretty worried about you."

"I have no choice but to try and figure this out."

Her head was pounding and her heart struggling to beat.

She swallowed a few drops of thick oily medicine and felt it move right into the painful places and get to work.

A battle above her waged, as her guardian Angels speared enemies with shafts of Light, before they reached Rain.

She rode back to her tipi and flipped through *The Thrill of the Chase*, figuring she might see something she had missed.

There was something with the twins and the mirror she did not understand, so she let it blur, the image on the page.

She saw two caverns and two chests reflected upon each other, but one dark the other light.

It made no sense to her.

She really hoped the chest was just in the cavern.

A few more horses had been placed in the pasture, a bubble of protection and another to confuse, was carefully arranged around the horses.

Taz, was given a potion that made him appear to be a fat black cat when being viewed.

CHAPTER XV

KEYS

"Exude gratitude. It transforms the day-to-day experience of illness and of life. Treasure the wonder of life... Become aware of your "guest status" in this brief moment of time and space. Be thankful. Exude gratitude. It heals."

Greg Anderson
Cancer, 50 Essential Things to Do

Night finally was lightening into day, and Rain thought,

"Today needs to be the day that I push forward."

Already several weeks had passed and the only thing she had gotten done was scramble to finish the push to get braced for a long and cold winter. The holiday season had descended upon the town and a blanket of snow softened the harsh edges of poverty and pushed it inside.

Just the other day at Big Medicine Springs, where she had taken to going lately, the owner, an Elder, with an outwardly crude and harsh shell, had made a joke about the weather.

"My thermometer said minus 12, I think I will take it outside tomorrow."

With all the frozen pipes, and the icy stares of cold outdoor pets and livestock, he was not far off.

Rain thought about the unusually cold weather and the fact that Kieran and Sarah had not left, she had been almost pushed to these pools that day. Soaking and enjoying the bejeweled spider webs dripping with diamonds of ice and hoar frost pearls, she heard someone slip in.

Glancing through the fog she saw a blonde head duck under and glide back out head tipped back and eyes closed.

She gave her a second, but then said, "Hey, how are you?"

They had met a few times at Symes.

"I did not know you came here too."

Rain was hoping her name would pop into her head, but not yet.

It did not matter, thought Rain, she might ask her in a minute. They began to talk, and the conversation turned towards their land and building project. The woman said something that really reined her attention in.

"My niece was poking around and found a small cave. We told her not to go in, but she did, and she found this really cool necklace with symbols all around it, you can tell it is really old, I know that I maybe should give it to the tribe, but I keep stuff I find."

She said cheerily.

Rain struggled to keep her face neutral.

This was the necklace that has the Dance of The Cavern of Heart mapped out on it, she dreamt about it often.

The woman yammered on, but Rain could hardly hear her.

She needed that necklace.

She said a hearty goodbye and made a mental note of the red pickup the woman drove.

Rain really wished she had asked her name, all the same, she would find where this necklace lay displayed and get it.

Sarah awoke from a restless night and did some planning of her own.

She could not take the way Kieran was spacing out, then snapping at her. He obviously was distracted and thinking about this woman.

The tall woman, with the piercing eyes had haunted her dreams since they had been there.

In the dreams she always lost her husband to the woman.

Sarah was an artist, so the looks and changing energy did not escape her, so her dreams seemed to simply be a warning.

Sarah quickly dressed and went downstairs to the lobby.

The heavier set woman, who worked in the mornings enjoyed gossip like her coffee.

If there were a scoop, she would know it.

Easing into the questions, Sarah complemented her.

It was true, that morning, the girl had taken the time to put on make up and was dressed up, so the extra cheer might help Sarah's cause, she thought.

"So, do you know that tall woman, skinny, calls herself Rain?"

"Yep," she grunted.

Maybe this was not going to be so easy.

"Well, what do you know?"

Sarah was a stranger, and this town did not divulge secrets to strangers.

"Not much, but I know she is outside right now."

Great, Sarah thought, just great.

Kieran was out there too.

Sarah hurried to get her suit, grabbing the one Kieran had told her he liked, she took two steps at once and scurried across the lot.

She was just in time to catch the tail end of a silvery laugh.

Kieran was staring at Rain in such a way that Sarah did not recognize, she knew right then, she would never get that look, it was suffocating, she tried to take a deep breath, pretended she was cheerful, and joined them in the pools.

Here was her opportunity to dig.

"So, Rain, tell me about yourself, and tell me how you two met?"

Rain caught the ice, but played the game.

"Oh, we met years ago, right here, it has been awhile,"

"I am many things, but right now I am looking for a treasure."

"I am on a quest to find answers, how about you?"

She turned the energy towards Sarah.

"I am an artist, we met in Missoula," she threw in.

"We are looking for..."

Kieran cut her off, "A new dig site."

Throwing her a look.

Curious, Rain thought.

She could feel her discomfort rising and made a stammering excuse, flashed one last glance at Kieran and Sarah and sprinted through the snow to the back pool.

She better find out what they really were up to.

She had the back pool to herself and the heat melted the tension away.

She practiced her movements she had developed to match the pieces she found.

They combined martial arts, yoga, dance, energy movement and breath with a Mayan greeting to the Sun.

"A way opens before us. All obstacles are released. Energy comes in and goes out to the World."

She visualized roots extending into the Earth and a flow of life energy coming through her, charging her, then giving it back to the Earth and repeated it in all four cardinal directions.

She felt the energy flowing and with gratitude eased into being present with the moment.

Across town, in the looking glass, an Elder sighed with relief, and allowed herself to rest for a moment.

She had it to herself.

Good, she was agitated and she needed to work on the dance.

She was having a hard time with a few of the moves at the end.

All of the pieces showed particular movements and made sounds when placed together and reflected.

They moved in a slow, almost imperceptible and repetitive pattern.

The moves needed extreme concentration, and the distractions were growing.

It was time to be able to complete the dance, if she did not hurry, it might be too late.

Gaia was losing ground on a daily basis.

There was only so much holding of Her that could be accomplished.

Rain would die before she let the Serpents win.

She might just do this, she thought, but she had already come so close to this, in her quest, and she knew she might have to sacrifice to win, and it might need to be her own body she sacrificed.

Breathing in Light, breathing out these train wrecked thoughts and feelings, she felt herself grounding in, allowing the flow of Gaia to come through her. Bowing left, then right, sweeping her hands in intricate gestures, she began the rhythmic breath, speaking the ancient language of movement, she opened the channels between worlds.

Just then, the gate creaked. Someone came in.

This person, she could feel, they joined the dance by witnessing and understanding her energy, and this knowledge had her eyes flying open, as nobody had joined her yet.

"Darn, I was right on the edge." She had to see who this was.

As her eyes adjusted, she was shocked to discover a face she remembered, but from when?

Their eyes locked in an old recognition of one another and they bowed in a Namaste.

Introducing themselves, in this life, "Cameron. And you are?" he asked in a deeply smoky voice.

She felt the response before she answered softly,

"Rain."

He extended his hand, she took it.

The grasp lingered, he held her gaze in a softly powerful way.

His eyes shimmered a chocolate promise of sensual enjoyment.

It had been a long time since Rain had let her guard down enough to let herself be touched, even with a glance as hot as this.

She was so lonely and even hungered for a hug.

Maybe she needed a distrac-

tion, yes, she did, as she heard the echoing laughter of Kieran from the other pool.

She allowed his hand to remain in hers long enough the intent and the response was clear.

They soaked and chatted in a familiar way.

"You want to grab a bite to eat later?" he asked.

"Sure."

She let it slide off her tongue, knowing she could chose to stop this at any time.

What harm would a bit of flirting and dinner do?

Enjoying his soft strength and easy conversation, Rain found herself drifting into the eyes of Cameron, trying to remember which life she had met him in before and why he might be here now.

She knew it was not coincidence and wondered which side he truly was on.

Rain knew she had to be careful, but she was lonely and was enjoying the company.

If he were truly Serpentine, she would figure it out.

You could tell, as the heart will not activate in a Serpentine, but stay cold and lifeless.

His eyes fired such heat and intensity, he could not possibly be.

She let herself drift into them, accepting the unspoken promise of much more to the night, if she would allow it.

"You want a massage?"

Rain chuckled at the obvious, but since she was feeling a need to be touched, she bit, "Sure" she said with a touch of challenge and invited him to her place.

Softly scented air and light that bounced in delicious patterns covered the warm cabin in an inviting mood.

Cameron ran his hands down her naked back, expertly loosening knots, inviting her deeper into her breathing and relaxation.

Rain was feeling vulnerable and allowed his touch to reach inside her soul. She felt an ignition of passion and threw out any thoughts of stopping.

He gazed deeply into her eyes, the brown reflecting the candlelight and showing the light of compassion.

He moved to her scalp, which was Rain's place of sensual ecstasy.

She would not be able to turn that off without satisfying it. She turned to him and invited a kiss that deepened with each taste and lick.

He knew just how to push and pull, both soft and demanding at the same time.

She felt the last strands of reason leave and dove into the evening with a screaming passion and heat that surprised them both.

When they had satisfied the curiosity and fed the flames inside each other until almost morning, finally Rain slept.

She slept without the dreams, without tossing and turning.

She slept like she had not since before she had lived in Salt Lake.

Rain guiltily remembered the past year, and knew though, she had needed to experience the deeply dark sexual energy Salt Lake City held, it brought her here, and more importantly, had awakened within her, the quest for treasure and truth.

She fell into the past memories.

Returning scratched up, dusty, cold and annoyed. Rain thought to herself, "If that goon had not ruined it, she would be loading up the VW with a bronze chest." Instead she warily watched a small hornet circle her leg and lamented her desperate desire to find the Chroma. She was tired of the tiny finds.

The fire crackled and soon the smoke drove the hornet on.

Warming up, she shivered internally.

Rain had already been so down and desperate, feeling that the taste of relief and hope were so strong, it kept her going.

Today was a tired day, so coming back empty handed, seemed to subtract yet another breath from limited supply and steal the hope.

The clues had lined up perfectly here, but someone had beaten her and had been waiting for her.

She had run and hidden in a small depression, near a dry creek bed and waited until almost dark to dash to the safety of an established campground.

They would not bother her around people.

Each time she had solved the riddle, so far, she had found pieces of a puzzle.

She hoped this link would show up.

She would have to go back to the blaze and go into the hole below it.

Rain guessed correctly, they had not found this key piece of the poem.

As soon as the day broke, she would go and see if the Chroma, or just another tidbit waited for her.

Right now she desperately needed to rest, and took a few drops of the precious oil keeping her alive.

Sighing, she absentmindedly

stroked the amulet pouch around her neck, and mentally recalled each item.

Most important was a small vial of an oily black substance.

It burned and raced to battle within.

She did not have much left, and tried to push aside her shortness of breath, by slowing down internally, and just appreciating where she was, which was beautiful.

She was near Lander, Wyoming, in the Sinks Canyon, camping by a rushing stream, that disappeared underground near where she lay resting.

It reappeared a half a mile below and to the left was a blaze upon the hill. The blaze was a horseshoe carefully placed in a cottonwood tree.

Just at the base of the bronze horseshoe, a tiny "ff" was inscribed so small, a magnifying glass had been needed to see it.

Just as she had seen this, she also heard a noise and ran, quietly to hide.

She had seen a man, carrying a huge rifle, trying to follow her tracks, but he getting frustrated.

She thought she had seen this man before, and struggled to remember where.

She already knew she was the only one who had figured out the double blazes, so was ahead of the game.

A mirror was needed or the perfect light at sunset reflecting to the spot where the small entrance hole was.

Forrest Fenn always left his clues in multiple layers.

When she returned in the morning, carefully making sure nobody saw her, she returned to the hillside.

She was right, they had missed it.

There was a tiny bronze box resting in the hole.

In it, was a small glass vial.

Wax protected the metal lid.

She melted it.

There appeared to be a paper with writing on it.

She got it out and read with her magnifying glass.

"Dear adventurous spirit, keep your eyes on the ground and keep searching. --ff"

She headed back to her camp and finished packing.

She was really tired that day and packing camp took longer than usual. Rain was worried, but kept going.

Though she was strong, at times she herself forgot she was ill.

After too long of ignoring symptoms and putting just enough healing into stay functioning, she had shut down several months before.

Rain knew she was being poisoned, as was all of Gaia.

Some felt it more than others.

A medicine built to be as powerful as the poison, highly effective and even more illegal, had blessedly made its way into her life.

There was a whole program meant to kill all intruders, yet as it was toxic, it took its toll.

Searching in the quiet had healing and maddening qualities.

Knowing that food and money were in short supply and returning empty handed meant back to the pages so to say.

She had fallen into an art, that

she was talented in, yet it had deep and dark sides and societal labels.

The blessing or gift to mend a broken heart, to touch places in the soul and body of another human, was, as all, a dichotomous gift.

Out of financial need, a young roommate had been found for the summer.

This one had not been carefully researched, as was the usual habit. Rain had ignored the feeling this young man might be trouble.

She wondered if she would ever finally listen to the voice all the time.

When the need for food and shelter became urgent, panic had set in.

His name was, Nathan, but he was called Silver Moon on the Backpages. Rain had never heard of this site, and was surprised after he posted an advertisement for her, her telephone exploded with texts responding booking appointments.

CHAPTER XVI

HOW A GIRL GETS BY

"When I turn into somebody nasty
I vow with all beings
to reflect on how it all happened
and uncover my long-hidden tail."

Robert Aitken
*The Dragon Who Never Sleeps: Verses for
Zen Buddhist Practice*

What Rain also did not know, was that the "Backpages" advertised thinly disguised prostitution and body rubs.

There were hundreds advertised.

The gentlemen arriving at her home, greedily grabbed.

Out of curiosity, shock, financial desperation and her own repressed desire, she played.

She did not have sex, but touched, let them sometimes touch and happily accepted $100 bills thrown her way. After a long period of being out of money and lack of desire to partake in society, it was a relief to have cash. She had seen both sides, extreme wealth and the poverty of the reservation.

At times, though, empowering, the cycles of abuse suffered in

the "appointments" was taking its toll on her.

She justified and enjoyed the moment, holding back at will, which became a dangerous game.

She had already been attacked two times and had men insist she "be" with them, and become extremely agitated at her refusal to date.

Her black belt had come in handy and she had only needed to use actual technique once, he regretted his decision.

"No punches," he had said after Rain unpinned herself and threw a complicated series of quick fists his way, landing just far enough away, and close enough he knew it would have hurt.

The rest was just a matter of give and take, acting and letting someone think they had the reins.

Those wise enough knew they were simply part of her dance, nothing more and nothing less.

She had regulars that she looked forward to seeing, and those she would consider dating.

The raw honesty was refreshing, the lack of games delightful and the no strings, ultimate control and financial gain made sense.

She was able to earn more in one hour than most in a day.

The risk was jail, public reviews about her, rape and worse.

It hardly seemed to be a fair trade off.

She would rather do this she thought, than be a slave to the system.

Rain learned to break the law years ago, working in healthcare.

She moved on to the darker and far more profitable world of the Backpages dot com out of desperation, but there was money and freedom.

She thought of her background and wondered if she would fulfill the prophecies or succumb to the forces as in lifetimes of burnings, hangings, stoning and general malediction of the people for a convenient answer. So many were caught in the web of lies, the air was thick with grayness and deceit, literally fogging Gaia and her people.

She thought surely the prophecies were wrong.

She had nothing to offer the world.

Darkness hung around her, hanging shame and guilt on her neck.

She let the hot tears fall onto folded hands and sent a wish out,

"Let me fulfill my destiny."

This was all that was needed to spark her deeper quest, the Council heard.

Rain breathed a huge sigh as she listened to Cameron snore softly, realizing how far she had come since Salt Lake.

She had barely made it out.

"I cannot believe there is a man in our bed," she said to Dasher, scratching his soft head.

He looked at her questioningly, "Can you be protected?"

"Yes, my friend, love is good, and I love you, but let's get real, two legged animals are my thing and I am lonely." She laughed, and hugged him.

There were still strongholds of magic left on Gaia.

Rain lived.

She had not felt the law after her for months now, just subtle tails of dark energy following her every move.

She had given up the money to heal and rest, find the answers to the quest.

After discovering the deeper meaning behind her desire to find the chest, Forrest Fenn hid, and for a time deny this, she had accepted the implications of her involvement.

It was life or death, an ancient battle between the forces of dark and light and their intimate entwinement.

She hoped, again, that this decision to indulge in the senses, would not set her back.

She had come to understand that the way the illness entered had to be taken into the body, willingly.

Either in food, fluids, water or by the promised safety of immunizations.

Feeling contented in touch, Rain pushed the anxiety away.

Thinking to herself though, she better take some medicine just in case.

This was too important to let her own needs get in the way.

She let the black oil burn her tongue and enjoyed, for a minute, the otherworldly feel that descended upon her.

Then, the pain began, she vomited and began to sweat, but she had to let it take the path to the places it needed to go.

An ancient medicine that had an awareness of itself and had been specifically recreated to help win the battle of the mysterious illness striking down young warriors of Light.

Some were not willing to go to depths of the soul and places of pain and discomfort it took you, and lost the battle.

Rain knew she must continue on.

Shivering, she slid into the past, remembering, all the while letting it go and realizing the lessons and necessities of our choices and the consequences that ensue.

She retched and the sweating started, but it did not last long.

This medicine built you up, rewired your system where needed, ate unhealthy cells and knew where to head to battle.

The first few minutes could be uncomfortable, but then the senses heightened, awareness alive and pain melted.

The more you let it work, the less it hurt in the process.

She watched the handsome man sleep, amused at the soft snore.

As she saw him stir more, she hid her notes and put some hot water on.

He awoke to a steaming mug of Montana Tea, Spiced Chocolate Chai.

He could see her outside doing the dance he had seen her do last night. He marveled at her. It was hard to label her, he thought.

She lived in a tipi, had features that looked somewhat native, but had long reddish wavy hair. She dressed in comfortable outdoor wear, wore a cowboy hat, moccasins, a huge amulet pouch, and a tie dyed scarf. The knife on her leg almost reached her knee.

Tall, lithe, graceful with long limbs.

He would not mess with her, he thought as her dance shifted into some complicated looking martial art moves, then back to a dance.

She was gorgeous; he well remembered her athletic and finely toned body. He thought he might see if she would come back to bed, but it looked like he might have to really convince her.

He sipped the tea and watched.

Too bad he would not be able to stay.

He enjoyed embodying a man and helping her let go.

He had missed her.

This body was a fine house.

He could be home, because his was far away.

CHAPTER XVII

DIGGING

"Sooner or later each of us will be nothing but leftovers of history or an asterisk in a book that was never written."

Forrest Fenn
The Thrill of the Chase

In Cabin 2, at Symes, Sarah fired off the email she knew would set the ball in motion for answers.

She had a friend.

A friend in high places, Sarah never dreamed even existed.

She was going to get to the bottom of this, and she would never let this woman come between them.

She would make sure of that.

One way or another.

The inbox chimed.

"That was fast," she thought.

When Sarah opened the inbox, she saw it was just a couple of spam emails and one from her Mom.

She would get to that, her Mom, very addicted to drama, probably just needed something, as usual.

She would call her later.

Sarah took a moment to revel in her bitterness and anxiety and then just like she has always done, she pretended.

Dressing in a flowing black skirt and high lace up leather boots, she added the silver bobs Kieran had given her yesterday.

She looked enticing she thought to herself.

Having had to fend for herself most of her life had given Sarah confidence. She knew she held power in her ability to pretend and knew her husband appreciated the effort.

Kieran strolled in and took a lingering glance at her.

He smiled and held a glint in his eye.

She was gaining ground.

Maybe it was not as serious as she thought.

After all, she could be misreading the energy.

Though, as soon as her contact returned her message, she would know. These people knew everything about everyone.

Sarah had a moment of doubt involving them, but ignored the sinking feeling she had.

She had hoped to be done dealing with them.

There was always a price.

This price she was willing to pay.

She took a moment to gloat as the screen lit up with her worst nightmare come true.

Here was a woman with a past, but one that included her husband.

As Sarah flipped through the documents on her computer, and time began to retrace itself with photos, reports, medical history and details of finances, friendships and worst, relationships.

Before her eyes were detailed pictures, video feeds documenting the not so distant past between the two, she fumed.

What she saw next explained the reason her husband was closed about having children.

He years before had had a vasectomy and was closed to the idea of even discussing it, making jokes and remaining firm, they would stay childless. The small grey cat Sarah loved so much, was pushing it in his eyes.

He liked to be free to go and explore.

His work as an archeologist demanded travel as well.

Well, he sure was hiding that he had already had a child.

One that died.

Here she saw Rain and Kieran on their final day together, mourning and then fighting.

She saw the pain, clearly reflected in his eyes, in the video footage captured.

It was hard to go anywhere on Gaia without being seen and recorded.

Her friends had not disappointed with the details.

Sarah now felt sick.

She also began to plot.

Hummingbird Rain Cassidy, was actually named Reagan Bauer, and came from an extremely wealthy and powerful family.

Her Mother's family was German and could be traced back to powerful roots.

Her Father's side was interesting.

They had been near Utah and had mixed in with the Ute Indians.

This side also was traced back to powerful beginnings.

They had been running and hiding a deep secret for centuries.

The original bloodline of Mary was held in their trust, and ancient documents protected, as well as stashes of gold, in the legendary mines of Carre-Shinob.

This information would cost.

Reagan, or Rain as she had named herself, as was the custom in the people she now called her tribe, the "Rainbows."

Generally thought of as misfits and outcasts, they had been some of the only ones not to be controlled by the technology and therefore a real threat.

What was useful to Sarah was the recent information.

The pages the law had submitted to the system, also always made it into her friend's reports.

They were thorough and Sarah felt she now knew enough to get this woman out of the way.

She knew the woman who provided her with the information would call on her soon enough and began to plot how she could use the secrets until then.

CHAPTER XVIII

TOLD

"Taking back responsibility to heal ourselves is the answer to our health-care crisis. As we learn to awaken within ourselves our natural self healing ability, we no longer feel confused...We gain confidence in our ability to heal ourselves...Great masters and teachers have all traditions have always spoken of a time when the secrets would come forth, a time when humankind would be able to comprehend the higher truths about life... That time is now here."

Dr. John Gray.
Power Healing

She felt them long before she saw them, they followed her at all times.

Had entered her home, had taps on all of her systems.

Then again, she lived in Utah, where the biggest "data" center was going in.

Some of her best customers came from there.

They told her, in confidence, things she should not know.

She felt much like Josie hearing Butch's tales.

These people were supposed to be on our side.

According to labels and law, the out was in and the law was out.

The only reason they waited to go after her was that one of the agents had predictably fallen for her and had convinced them she might be of future use in the deep investigations ongoing in Salt Lake City.

She had by ill fate, wound up working in two of the hottest spots for body rubs and under the deepest undercover investigations.

She had managed to meet two women deeply involved in the sex trade and deeply in bed with the police.

She had stories of hookers and heroin all the while with a pretty healing cover.

The hypocrisy in the city was astounding to her and disturbing as she had been privy to such unwanted information.

The things she knew could topple several local dynasties and ruin multiple lives.

These things she knew.

She also knew she would die one day and it was going to be sooner rather than later, if she did not get her life in order and get out of there.

First, though, she had to find the chest that Forrest Fenn had placed somewhere in the Rocky Mountains, above 5,000 feet and at least 8.25 miles north of the eccentric man's home.

Rain needed to meet him and look in his eyes.

He had become decidedly wary, and felt her intensity as well as her feeling his energy trails.

He must have wondered who this strange and lonely woman was and why she wanted to meet him but had agreed to, after she sent him her best photos of herself and left a gift.

She was striking and used this to her advantage; it had not been in vain.

It happened to countless hunters, they became infected with a desire to find the chest, entranced with the man who put it out there, wrapped up in the history and future.

She had touched his heart and he wanted to know her.

She suspected an ancient Voodoo curse placed upon an item in the chest, perhaps unbeknownst to Forrest himself.

This is what the curse said.

The one who opened it, had their soul stolen.

The chest, called the Chroma, in ancient prophesies and to those dreaming of it, floated between reality and worlds and was caught in a vortex of time.

A tribal Elder had told her of this, years before the chest had even been hidden. She had been told of her involvement and that she was to find it, to help put balance back in the needy world.

She had forgotten the story and blown it off as false, until Andy, a customer, had told her he was searching for it, she remembered the Elder pulling her aside years ago.

At first, Rain wondered what the draw was, after all, money did not mean happiness and all the gold in the world could not pull her to it.

But she was dreaming of an ancient necklace that held the secrets that humanity needed to change, she felt it calling her in her dreams.

Finding the chest had always been her life's mission, the path had just been buried in lies and cover-ups.

She began to remember the stories she was told and the whispers she heard.

The one who had pulled her aside one dark evening, twenty-five years ago, drunkenly slurring,

"You're the One to finds it or dies trying, keep it together so it does not fall apart," he slurred.

Another had come and pulled him away, angrily glared at Rain, and shook his rattle for half an hour in his car.

Rain had watched, puzzled, she blew the whole thing off.

Weird things happened to her all the time and she thought it just another reason to leave this town she had been made to call home.

Looking for the chest had started because she was curious and battling an illness eating at her, she felt an urgent need to find it, as the money could buy her health.

There, also, was this deep calling within to help and to stand up as a warrior in these dark times.

She had to be well.

After lifetimes of defeat, it was time to put the dark forces of greed to rest. She had yet to face the biggest challenges.

Andy, his cover was banking, had come to see her seven months previous.

Before the session was over, he had disabled his intricate wiring, and held his fingers to his lips.

Rain had reminded him so much of his mistress that he could hardly breath. Ivana had been a Russian intelligence officer and had been exposed to toxic levels of radiation.

She died at age 28, his heart had not mended.

He had not expected the tender loving touch and open heart at her table, after years of deadness, feeling a spark was a miracle.

He fell prey to her charm, saw the intelligence and the barely contained tears.

He had come in expecting to be the one who fooled her radar.

He was well-trained.

Instead, she pierced the armor of his heart holding his hand in hers, he had expected those hands to be locked in steel, yet he could not stop himself from wanting her desperately.

Her judgment about giving happy endings to customers, was enough of a shield, he thought.

He had seen her pictures, all of them, and knew it would be hard to not at least feel attracted.

A solid handful of officers had tried to fool her, but their energy gave them away.

There were three types that came to her: cops, creeps and cool.

Rain could fit any variety into one of those.

She had about seen them all now, she thought.

Andy was comfortable on the table, his breathing relaxed, the drape on. He glanced over to see if she had taken off any of the fine layers of colored skirts and scarves she wore.

No.

The room smelled delicious.

The jasmine, sandalwood and rose combination she had on drifted by his nose.

She invited him to take three deep breaths, in through his nose and out through his mouth.

"Ground your roots deeply into the Earth, visualize an extension of yourself going deeply into the center."

"When you feel this connection, allow it to rise up into your body, let the energy flow through you, in a clockwise circle, let it move around, remembering your perfection, remembering how loved you are."

"I invite all of Andy's guardians and Angels to be present and for his own highest healing to be activated."

He struggled to stay alert, rubbing his eyes.

She noticed and invited him deeper into a trance.

She began to sweep the energy over him, and open his minor and major chakras.

When she touched his hand he jumped at the energy jolt and his eyes opened in time to see the love she reflected to him.

She mirrored the Love of Source, he felt it.

She reminded him again he was perfect and made of love, and let the music build the energy into a chaotic place, then back to a still point.

He had indicated, by grabbing her legs and rubbing, trying to touch higher, he wanted release.

She sensed he was law, but that he did not care, he was lost, so she obliged.

She had those who she knew would never tell what happened behind those doors, no matter who they worked for.

She was a touch surprised when he asked her out for a coffee.

Her policy was not to mix her worlds, so she said

"No."

"Come on, it is the end of the World Friday, meet me Saturday."

She laughed. She liked him.

"OK, ten in morning, Saturday December twenty-second, at the Greenhouse Effect."

So, it began.

This cop had an interesting story and Rain decided, yes, she would take advantage of his interest and learn as much as she could.

They began to meet in secret, he taught her to evade the tails, how to fool the surveillance.

She taught him how to love again.

He began to share about a treasure quest he was on, it took a hold of her and triggered the memory of a deeper search.

CHAPTER XIX

THE CLIENTS

"When I am moved to complain about others
I vow with all beings
to remember that karma is endless
and it's loving that leads to love."

Robert Aitken
*The Dragon Who Never Sleeps: Verses for
Zen Buddhist Practice*

She readied herself for her appointment and prayed he was not with the law.

She scrubbed, buffed, perfumed and fluffed, took a peek out the window at the white SUV waiting to follow her.

She had no doubt that with all the technology, they could tell things about her, she did not know.

He came in swaggering with the glee of a young child who stole bubble gum, never getting caught.

She could tell "not law," but had an air of dominance and danger.

She took a deep breath, swallowed her pride and fear and stepped into the room.

He proudly displayed himself upon the table, a dare.

She seductively covered him with silks and established her soft dominance.

She dimmed the lights and took time to surround the room with energy, grounding her roots in.

Despite the thought that some had coming, the work was extremely beneficial and needed.

Within the sexual energies lying within each person untapped and feared, answers to the great questions rested, Rain understood that.

She knew he was not expecting healing, but saw him relax into breath and rhythm.

He began to try and grab onto her, she softly moved out of the way, strategically placing body parts for maximum touch and minimal reaching ability to her own privates.

She knew to teach them about their own power was a great gift, but they usually wanted more.

They wanted to possess her, to control, to dominate and they became frustrated when it did not progress.

Several times a physical challenge had ensued.

She had been tossed around and had to let the man know that under no circumstance was he getting out unscathed.

She preferred the soft and subtle dance of energy and loved providing comfort and love.

She did not enjoy being grabbed at, considered a prostitute or risk her freedom.

The bills needed to be paid and she had to have time to rest.

To gain freedom though, she was paying an expensive debt that was taking a toll.

She was anxious and on edge, and had been feeling physically worse.

Her head throbbed, but she ignored it and smoothed out the silk sheets.

She liked to make sure all of the senses received pleasurable information.

She had another client, a repeat.

He worked at the Data center and always brought her good coffee and told her about the workings of the place.

He was polite and never pushed her, but enjoyed his session moaning in pleasure as Rain ran her hands softly down his limbs as healing music played.

She could see herself reflected in the mirror and hardly recognized the sexy woman.

She angled so he could enjoy the view too and got to the business of why he was there.

Why most of them were.

She expertly squeezed and drew long strokes picking up the pace when he was ready.

By the time the men were ready for release, it was usually easy.

"Sweet Jesus," he moaned too loudly.

Rain had been studying the male anatomy and had tried a prostate massage on him.

It had worked.

She shushed him and held him tightly, then softly cleaned him with warm, wet cloths, gave him privacy, a raw chocolate treat and a cup of hot peppermint tea.

He kissed her cheek and headed out to his government issued rig, reported back to his secret office, in the huge underground data-mining center.

She was legitimate.

Rain had a treasure box out there to find and was ready to go looking again, this was her last appointment for a while, she needed to leave the city.

Maybe she would feel better again on the road.

It seemed to help to be out of Salt Lake.

Her car was packed already.

She just had to get through this, it was not like this body part had never touched her hands, but today the needy greediness was bothering her.

She was riding with the windows down, music shockingly loud, close to Wyoming, enjoying the solitude when she saw the surveillance van behind her.

They probably would drop off in Wyoming, but just to be sly, she crossed several lanes and exited.

Laughing to herself, Rain picked a new way to her destination and drove on musing with thoughts.

She was fed up.

The rage and injustice of it all was brewing to a dangerous place of quiet. She found herself simmering with a pride and finding the rod behind her spine return from its broken land of abuse and lies.

To find the answers meant looking for more and she knew nothing, getting to the top of one mountain meant there was the next to climb. These realizations had brought her peace and the motivation and energy she needed to get out of Salt Lake City.

She was so glad to be gone and still struggled with the shame of it all.

Why would she be able to help?

Who was she, really?

Rain had been given a gift, the way out, but only by going through the deep dark would she be able to see herself in the Light she needed to.

It had been Andy who had helped her escape, just in time.

The plan had been to kill her, by injecting tiny particles into her blood, letting the disease they had planted, spread and kill her.

By all appearances, until it was too late, everything would look fine.

The retching, pain, constant weakness and heavy fatigue set in fast.

Somehow, Rain had gotten out, but only with lots of help.

A few weeks before she left, she had a modeling job out by the lake.

The pictures had helped her have the money she needed to rest.

She laughed as she thought about what had happened.

It was another reason she knew she needed to leave.

They had finished the shoot.

"That was fantastic doll, it is a wrap."

"Let's get going."

They hopped in his white Prius and began driving.

"So, I am headed out of town, but would love to get a copy of the shoot."

He was a friend, so she hoped he did not mind.

"Yeah, it will take me a bit, but you can. Where are you going?"

"Looking for that treasure box."

"Oh?"

"Yeah, a box filled with gold. I am going to find it. Anyone can look. I have gotten close. I am going to meet the man who put it out there."

He looked strangely out at her.

A few minutes passed in silence before he said,

"I have been dreaming about a bronze box, called the Chroma."

Rain paled.

"You dream about it? What?"

He looked her over.

"That a girl and an older man find it. It is being hidden by the twins and moved in between times and worlds."

"The twins are worried about who finds it, and their intent."

"What does it look like?"

"The landscape is desert, like New Mexico. They go down into a big rock. A kiva. The box is in this rock. There is water in front of it and low mountains behind it."

"The time shifts in my dream, so it is hard to tell."

He stared again.

"The girl looks like you and is wearing a hat. The older man is southern."

"Tell me more about what it looks like."

Just then a huge red truck bore down on them.

Rain panicked.

She thought maybe it was a client who had seen the photo shoot and was chasing them.

She was losing it.

The huge truck pulled alongside them and was waving at them frantically.

He sped up and they fell back.

Not for long.

They were back beside them and gesturing.

Rain dared look harder.

They were pointing to the roof and made the sign for telephone.

"Did you put your phone on the roof?"

"Oh, shoot, I did."

They waved back at them in thanks and pulled alongside the freeway.

"Oh, that is funny, the video camera is on."

They watched as the sky flew by.

You could just see the edge of the truck and then hear them when they stopped and got out, laughing.

Rain stored the new tidbits about the box in her brain, hoped he could tell her more and enjoyed the rest of the drive back to Salt Lake.

It had been a long day, and she needed to finish packing.

CHAPTER XX

TRACKS

"When I panic at losing my bearings
I vow with all beings
to acknowledge the error is panic,
not losing familiar ground."

Robert Aitken
*The Dragon Who Never Sleeps: Verses for
Zen Buddhist Practice*

Rain woke drenched in sweat, she wished she knew what time it was.

It was hard to tell from the light, if it was close to breaking yet.

Though she had chosen this solitude, the in-between hours were the hardest.

She felt the chill, the fire had gone out, and she rolled out of bed to get it going again.

She really hoped the sweating was unrelated to the sweats that she had all last year.

Maybe it was just because when she had gotten home the night before, there had been fresh boot tracks outside of her small cabin.

They had circled by the wood shed and around the house.

She could see where they had looked in each window.

Whoever it was, Rain thought, was not professional.

The boot prints were not small, but not big enough to guess which sex.

It had bothered her.

After the time she had spent hiding, running and looking over her shoulder, she had just about had it with worrying.

So, she let it pass, but maybe her dreams were telling her something her body was manifesting into sweats.

She certainly could not remember the dream.

She would see who it was with her seeing bowl, she decided.

This had been gifted to her by her grandmother before she died.

The rose quartz bowl, with the tourmaline bottom, filled with water, showed answers.

What Rain saw was disturbing.

It was Kieran's wife, Sarah.

"What the hell,"

This woman was trouble, what was she thinking snooping around?

Rain had been so good to stay away from them, but she supposed the woman had felt it.

Rain could hardly blame her.

Kieran often was secretive, which to her, had invited curiosity.

Strangely enough, she felt a new connection to the short haired, attractive woman.

She was glad she had looked, and now got ready to go snooping herself.

Rain dreamed again of the necklace that sang.

It paired with the other objects to show her how to finish the dance to open the secret cavern, by the river.

She was sure it was the one up near the house.

In her dream, she remembered placing it in a small cavern and set a memory activator in it.

It was on a tiny ledge and should have been invisible in its resting spot.

The child who found it must be a young Light Worker.

She was seeing how she would still need to break her codes and steal it. She needed the necklace to sing the song, so she could do the dance.

Rain headed to the library next and researched the property and house. The listing had never been taken down, a year later.

The pictures were detailed, and Rain guessed the huge mantle might hold pretty treasures.

The approach would be wooded and she could get in and out without being noticed.

She knew just how and when.

Rain had seen the red truck leaving the hardware store yesterday.

As far back as she could, Rain followed.

She did not need to go far.

The truck turned onto a lane that was a dead end, with only a few houses.

Rain turned around.

She would go back later.

Rain felt kind of bad, as she liked the woman, but this was no reason not retrieve the song key.

She had learned her name was Helen and her husband Brad.

They were new to the area as well, and had only bought the house about a year ago.

They were doing renovations and lots of improvements.

They had found the small cavern by accident.

She had told the young girl not to go in.

Rain had learned quite a bit about them by listening to their conversation in the pool.

She had been pretending to drift and just let them fill her ears with good information.

They were planning to go to see family in Missoula soon and were figuring out when.

Like many people in sleepy Hot Springs, they were likely to decide on a whim rather than planning.

She pulled up by the country lane and cut her car engine off.

Stepping out into the cool air, Rain had a moment of doubt as to how she would explain herself if seen, but pushed on anyway.

It was a perfect time for them to run to Missoula and Rain was taking a chance they had left.

The necklace shimmered in her mind.

The ancient pieces falling into perfect place when worn by the One.

She finally believed with all of her heart that she had lived many lifetimes to be right here, right now and that she was the One.

The prophesied One, meant to awaken the Dragon, of ancient lore, lying below the Mountains stretching from Hot Springs all the way through Missoula and up into the Bitterroot Valley, down to the desert.

The Dragon lay waiting for her.

She could feel herself flying in wind upon Her back again and began to glow within, finding that place of still and timeless perfection that is carried deep within our hearts.

She felt her breath slowing as she reached the edge of their property.

They had no idea what they had in there.

The property was perfect for what she was doing, as soon as you crested over a small knoll, you were not visible. Rain reached this place and took a moment to listen. It was quiet and the truck was gone.

Rain was careful to step only in places where the snow had melted so she would not leave prints.

Approaching the house, she listened again, then went to the garage, which was unlocked.

There were a few cars, most looked in disrepair.

One, a shiny black Saab, was out of place, but come to think of it Rain had seen it around once.

It had seemed out place to her then, but now knowing, since they had come from elsewhere, it made sense.

Rain checked the door, and was pleased it was unlocked.

She rifled for a minute and was puzzled when the registration was under a name she did not recognize, Katherine Haynes, but Rain had other things to worry about.

She needed the necklace that was in the house.

Chances were something was unlocked and after circling the well-chinked log cabin, Rain found a window open in back.

It was encouraging the doors had been locked, as most people left their things unlocked here, it meant they had gone to Missoula for sure.

Rain had awhile to look, but it did not take long as her heart began to light up and she felt the pull of the ancient music stones beckoning her with a soft tune carried across the wind.

She let her senses relax and followed it.

What she did not immediately sense was "Katherine Haynes" who was a scout and messenger for Shakira.

She had been in Hot Springs as well, and knew of the key code necklace, and she knew it would not work without Rain.

This Serpentine had taken on the form of a woman with dark hair she wore pulled back in a ponytail.

She wore business suits and drove the Saab.

She was good at infiltrating people's lives and was pleased to have been called on, again, by Sarah, who thought she was with the underground mafia surrounding the ever growing black market of illegal adoptions.

Sarah had looked into it, though she knew Kieran would not agree.

This is where she had learned about what kind of information could be obtained, for just a few dollars and an eternal debt.

They had hoped the humans would not get this far, as the propensity to destroy the planet and themselves had been enough.

They had not worried too much about the prophesies, as Rain did not seem capable, they thought, of bringing the change needed to awaken the magic to save the planet.

Now, though, if the humans remembered and uncovered Atlantis and Ahomea, the Serpents would be forced to find another planet to take.

They were about out of options.

Tension in the ship increased.

Shakira ordered more chemical sprays, and since so many were refusing vaccines, she ordered a widespread release of the drones to infect people.

Rounding the corner, Rain sensed something was off.

As she dropped into stillness, the sounds around were easier to distinguish from feelings.

She felt a deep cold that she had begun to associate with the Serpents.

She had one last bit of cloaking she had gotten off a vendor, wise to magic disguises strong enough for fooling the best of the Serpent guards and used it.

Pulling it out of the small vial, Rain swallowed.

Effectively surrounding herself in a cloud of No Thing, relishing the inner peace this brought with the ability to hide.

Katherine was patient, as though Rain had sensed her, she could not see her.

She had to stop this magic from getting out.

Rain made her way around the house, resting her eyes on a mantle, she saw it.

It shimmered in response to her energy.

It was giving her away, Rain quickly grabbed it and stuck it a velvet bag, but it continued to glow.

Just as she was getting out the door, she felt the cool breath hiss in her ear

"Got you."

Rain turned to face her enemy, and was surprised to see an image of herself coming at her, and realized the Serpent had used a shadow-revealing spell.

Rain would be fighting herself and her mind.

Any fears, any lack of presence will feed this angry shadow of herself, allowing it to capture her true nature, resting in her heart.

She would have to fight her own worst enemy, her shadow, the mind side, out of control.

Fears began to cloud her vision, Rain felt the collective pain of Gaia coming through her, as she fell to the ground.

The necklace began to vibrate in the bag and rose, on its own, tired of being still, it was ready for action.

It was simply an extension of the Dragon, a Green Love breather, meant to be activated by her, in this time.

It rested in between worlds, but was called on now, again.

The bloodline of the original Light Workers, rested in her, hibernating in the stones of the ancient portal opener.

It shimmered and rose above, flashing a brilliant opalescent light, which sent Katherine back to her ship.

Deep in the center of the dark and ever-growing dilapidated ship, they met and discussed how to move forward.

"There is magic from the old world trapped in the stones of that necklace."

"It appears to light just for this one."

"We will have to use her to get it to work."

"We still need to know how to get into Atlantis, and destroy the last magic."

"I have not waited around this ugly little planet, with its stupid humans, for this long to lose."

"Get down there and fill that town with us, she will not know what hit her."

Across town, Iris Thorugh, woke from her sleep and nudged her partner, James.

"Did you feel that?"

Yes, he had, and he knew what it meant.

"That nosy do-gooder is ruining it for us."

She has the key.

Getting out her communication device, Iris was the name she had picked. She was an orator and a healer of the Serpentine, sent to instill the disease in as many people as she could convince to follow her and "see her."

She advertised as a spiritualist, spreading the dark with each greedy client she fed off.

The first night Rain had been in the pools, they had been there, ready.

"She has it."

"Yes," screamed the Queen,

"I know!"

The ship was in an uproar.

For the first time in centuries, they felt they might not actually steal this planet so easily.

They had simply had to wait out the drama of the human mind to play itself out.

They were not bound by time as the humans, but more witnessed, as entertainment, humankind destroying one another with the mind. Now the prophesied one had the key.

Iris needed energy for this fight, so she called one of her "clients" and scheduled an appointment.

This man had a huge sexual charge and she enjoyed feeding off of it, his drama surrounding a prostitute.

She plugged her invisible cord into him and began in her sweet voice, the one she reserved for manipulating humans

"I just love the freedom sexual liberation gives, don't you Senator?"

Iris Thorugh purred seductively, pouring him a glass of water infused with the sleeping potion devised to keep humans unaware and in the drama and divisions.

So many were on the verge of waking, they had taken to spraying the air with chemicals designed for apathy and toxicity.

She felt her cold energy grow with the false light of sexual charge, she needed her strength to keep Rain in check.

She rubbed his back and began stripping the rest of her blue string bikini off.

Sliding and slipping, rubbing herself and taking his energy to a deeply dark and sexual place.

There was no love involved.

CHAPTER XXI

FALSE PROPHETS

"When something tears at the fabric
I vow with all beings
to come forth with the voice of no-source
and show it cannot be torn."

Robert Aitken
*The Dragon Who Never Sleeps: Verses for
Zen Buddhist Practice*

Just as Rain was opening her door, the phone rang.

She was tired and did not feel like talking, but picked it up.

It was Iris.

"Hi, how are you? What are you doing today? I have a client who was hoping for a four hand."

"Iris, I am not seeing clients, I told you this."

"Oh, it is all legit, it is the Senator I told you about."

Rain did not care, she could feel the charge and the temptation to earn some money.

She was running low, but did not want to risk the darker places, nor the trouble this woman brought.

Rain had been careful to stay out of jail.

She knew what a two-hour Tantric "massage" meant.

She never had slept with her clients, this woman did, for the same price.

When Iris's irritation came through, her sweet demeanor cracked enough to hear the malice in her reply,

"Well, whatever, see you later?"

Rain had started to wonder about them.

They had been in the pools her first night, talking about Salt Lake City.

Rain had fallen for it, and talked to them.

They knew enough about her to be dangerous and felt that way anyway.

Just last week, Rain had caught a glance of such anger and hatred in Iris's eyes, she knew she was hiding something.

Rain was beginning to think Iris Thorough might be really dangerous and she was worried.

Rain went to the library and did some digging.

What she found out about this woman was disturbing.

She had been to jail and ran her own organization, she claimed to be a minister.

It seemed to be a legitimate thing, until one dug deeper.

Then the bad reviews and stories behind her followed.

There was an active warrant for her arrest.

Clients complained about her sexual energy versus the ancient Tantric energy, Where she had taught, they said it was a brothel.

Rain had worked at a studio she had been told was legitimate.

These were friends of Iris's.

The woman who ran the place had two identities.

She was a well-known madam.

It had taken Rain several weeks to figure it out, find a new place and get away from the women and their clients.

She already was wrapped up in it though.

The association with the studio was enough for the reviews to pop up that,

"She is at a known, full service spot, she has not been "full service" before, but it is worth a try."

Rain also found heroin hidden there.

She was organizing and came across a cosmetic pouch.

"I wonder who is diabetic?"

She thought.

Then she saw the blue tourniquet and an aluminum ball.

She had dropped the case and wiped it off, wondering if it was the Reiki Master who was there most days.

Come to think of it, she was extremely skinny, had bad teeth, and her moods oscillated.

"Yes, it is her."

Rain thought sadly.

The woman was in her late sixties and clients who came to Rain talked. She would do release for three hundred and fifty dollars, sex for more.

And she would brag about being legitimate and informing every client ahead of time, it was not release.

What a place.

She had gotten her own working space after this, and this made it nicer.

She had hoped to be done with these people, but they were glad to know where she was.

She had been seen as a threat to both legal business and the illegal sides of the place.

She did not approve of the

"girls" and wanted no association with gum smacking prostitutes named Lilly or whatever.

That she knew about the illegal operations was seen as a loose end.

How loose.

To be determined.

CHAPTER XXII

STOLEN IN TIME

"To him that overcometh will I give to eat of the
hidden manna, and will give him a white stone, and
in the stone a new name written, which no man
knoweth saving he receiveth it."

Revelation 2:17

Resting in her tipi, she looked at the necklace.

It was simple.

The symbols touched a place inside.

Claws hung from the middle and small animals were carved into the stones, alongside the symbols.

The necklace shimmered and sung a low tune in the bag, daring her with bold displays of magic.

Rain needed to get it to be less obvious.

She thought she had found the missing song code.

She knew it did not sing for anyone.

It was singing.

Well, she sighed, I guess I really need to do this now.

"But someone will feel you, please be quiet."

As if hearing, the necklace quieted down.

Rain was not sure what she should do now, and took a moment to check in with her animal companion and guardian.

Letting his soft fur soothe her and help drop the mind, she just felt, in gratitude, that she really might be able to do this, and to be rested, finally.

Shakira watched and knew for sure she could not kill Rain, yet.

Dasher growled a low and inaudible howl as he sensed the Queen watching.

"Back off you Serpent scum."

Beams of golden light shot out from his eyes as he watched and guarded.

Shakira let out a slow hiss as a return warning.

"Watch yourself, I am."

Laughing, she masked herself.

Across town, the new couple returned home.

She did not notice it missing, at first, but had taken to looking at it.

It seemed to be speaking to her.

She was losing it in this town.

The boarder, Katherine, they had taken in was gone, as was her stuff.

She had not even paid this month.

Walking to the mantle.

She saw some things tipped over and noticed something was not right.

Her necklace was gone.

"Honey, somebody has been in here. They stole that necklace Tara found."

"You want me to call the sheriff?"

"No, you know we should have turned it in, it was pretty tribal."

"Is anything else gone?"

He walked in with his rifle.

"I will look around."

"Well, I guess it is just gone."

"Now who would have taken it?"

She remembered talking to the girl in the pools about it, who had seemed pretty interested, but that girl was a loner, and did not seem like she would break into a home and steal.

It was probably young tribal members.

"Oh well, it ain't the first thing somebody stole from me. Just let it go, put that away, nobody is here. Let's go soak."

CHAPTER XXIII

SKELETONS

"When dissension comes up in the family
I vow with all beings
to suggest we get in our loving
Who knows if we'll be here next month?"

Robert Aitken
*The Dragon Who Never Sleeps: Verses for
Zen Buddhist Practice*

The phone shrilled an alarm, and screamed to be picked up.

"Reagan," her Mom bellowed across the line, "Your Father has had a heart attack."

When was the phone good news that late at night?

"Well, Mother, is he alive?"

"Yes, you need to come home right now."

They had moved east, to Boston.

"You know I cannot."

"Why, Reagan, why do you do this to us?"

Rain let her anger boil over for just a second.

Had her Mom forgotten? Refusing to show up, even when Rain was deathly ill.

It was the height of the social season and there were parties to attend, she had not had time, she said.

Well, Rain did not have time for either of them and swallowed a lump.

Above, the Queen watched, pleased Rain was getting wrapped up in her head and emotions.

They could plot while she was distracted.

"Mother, I cannot come, I am not going to argue with you."

There was part of Rain that was not surprised her infallible and powerful Father had succumbed to heart issues.

His was cold.

How else could he behave the way he did?

Fuming, Rain hung up.

She was not going.

Her Father had heard and worried his daughter's temper would get in the way of what she needed to do.

He had been the hardest to convince to let her find her own path.

When it had been time to send her away, he had cried, alone, but kept a stoic face.

There had been times when he had wanted to intervene and rescue his daughter, but knew she had chosen to walk her own road.

He watched from a distance and was in contact with his family in the area. Though they stayed away from Rain, it was required for her to fulfill the prophecy. She was always watched.

Each swing of temper recorded, each moment of clarity and vision celebrated.

He had kept his Seeing bowl and watched from afar.

His heart had been bothering him, and the stress of his daughter ill and struggling, and his inability to help had pushed him into a full myocardial infarction.

He had survived, and in his weakened state had more time to See and Watch.

He sent prayers and energy and had faith his daughter could continue to bring the light needed.

She would find the items she needed to get into the chambers, see what she needed and then continue on with the most dangerous part.

She would need to be well and ready for a battle.

He understood her anger and sent love in return.

Reagan's Mom was in a frenzy.

She had three parties she was in charge of and her husband's failing health had disturbed her routine.

She radioed the ship from her private chambers, she had insisted on having built.

"She seems to be emotional."

"Yes, keep calling and bringing up her feelings, promise help, but make her ask."

"Feed her issues and keep her angry with her Dad."

"Yes, my queen."

Said the blender in Margarethe Bauer.

They had sent her away.

She had been sixteen.

It was supposed to be a healing place based on Native American philosophy, Outward Bound and the Twelve Steps.

What occurred was unforgivable.

They were isolated and controlled by the whims of a madman.

The place had sunk itself and the man had made his amends to a group of people who were not made up of those who had endured.

It had been just down the road from home and she had been one of the only kids from Montana.

It had been her Grandfather's idea, but then he needed her out of the way after she started fighting back.

He had been abusing her every time the family had returned East.

The last time, Rain had been ready for him when he entered her room.

She had left no visible marks and he quickly retaliated by funding her "reform."

Since there had seemed to be some value in learning about survival, choices, consequences, honesty and all the room in between, her family here consented too.

The school was one of those that put the kids through great physical and mental challenges.

When you were finished fearing for your life, puking up bile and realized they really were the way out, you followed.

Many nightmares have been born in the woods of Northwest Montana.

Rain thought and felt this deeply, sinking, her jaw worked in tight motion, chewing on bitterness.

She felt a deep weight rest on her, pulling her downwards.

She remembered there were others who had been there.

Taking her thoughts outside lessened the pounding rage.

Coming home had stirred up buried memories, her shadow was working hard to swallow her.

At this rate, she would fail, drowning in thoughts, memories, feelings and the past.

She felt something stirring, realized it was the frog stone she had found near Thermopolis in Wyoming.

It was singing in a barely audible tone.

The necklace, resting in the purple bag began to respond.

The dreamy tones soothed Rain and she let the tightness fall into the ground.

The sounds from her bag chimed.

The song was not complete, she still was searching for the box.

She was close.

Not as close as she thought.

She drifted and dreamed.

Digging in the gravel pit, for a whole day, had been her punishment for not following some rule or another.

In her dream, she ran away.

She made it down the fifteen miles of Blue Slide, to the bridge at Trout Creek.

She walked down highway 200, towards Sandpoint.

When cars passed, she hid in the woods.

They all knew not to pick up teenagers on the road, around here.

At the same spot, every time, she walks back, fully into the woods.

She is walking so quietly.

She is an Indian.

She rounds a corner and lets out a gasp as she sees the big brown bear. The bear stops eating, looks her in the eyes, and asks

"Are you there yet?"

"Where? Where?"

The bear is always gone.

CHAPTER XXIV

THE THRILL

"So I decided to fill a treasure chest with gold and jewels, then secret it—leaving clues for any searcher willing to try. It was a perfect match of mind and moment."

Forrest Fenn
The Thrill of the Chase

Throwing the book with irritated frustration, Kieran figured it had to be more than just the chest.

He and Sarah had been looking for a treasure chest that Forrest Fenn hid.

He had been lucky enough to have been invited to Mr. Fenn's San Lazaro ruins for a special presentation.

A new artifact had been uncovered and Mr. Fenn excitedly had described another piece, one he had placed in a chest he secreted in the Rocky Mountains.

Twenty-two turquoise discs adorned a simple silver bracelet.

It held special power.

Forrest also spoke of a necklace that sounded strangely familiar to the young archeologist.

The new piece, Mr. Fenn thought, had been traded from the same area and perhaps was connected to the Navajo Rainbow Bridge legends as well. Kieran found himself winding into tight knots of anxious tension.

The same stomach-sinking feeling he had around Reagan, or Rain as she called herself now, she was back.

He had thought that when he met Sarah, he had found the one who could replace that.

He had been wrong.

The last time he and Rain had been together, he remembered with a sickening dread, he had buried his own heart in there with that baby.

He swallowed this sickening feeling, and asked about this chest.

"Well, I have placed it somewhere north of Santa Fe, in the Rocky Mountains, for anyone willing to look. Here, I have a copy of my book." He signed it, "Keep your eyes on the ground, ff."

Kieran gratefully accepted and began his quest to find the chest.

He was very interested in the turquoise bracelet and the legend of the twins.

The ancient necklace Mr. Fenn described sounded hauntingly familiar.

He flashed on a dream and saw a smoky hallway, someone running and holding a necklace.

His daydream was interrupted when Sarah asked him if he was ready to leave, they needed to go home.

"Well, is there a bronze chest filled with millions in our jeep, yet?" She sighed, he was not going anywhere.

She would have to think of something else. At least he still seemed to be thinking just about the chest and not the woman he was lying about.

They had followed the clues in the poem and it had led them here, of all places, where he had met her.

He remembered the night well.

It had been drizzling, but the light shone through, just as the sun fell behind the sky for the night, the colors dropping hints of luscious promises of tomorrow.

He had been daydreaming about going trekking and had nearly run over her.

Choice words had flown, but when their eyes met, neither could deny the force between them.

It did not need words.

They both had flashes from lifetimes of being together and could understand the language of their souls resonating in frequency with a higher purpose.

The moment lasted through lifetimes of pictures and images, but took only a few in linear time.

The pull was irresistible and only great pain had caused them to separate.

He could not stand the emotions welling up, he did not feel in control, and did not like the way he automatically responded to Rain.

He loved Sarah, but not like the painful way that he loved Rain, in dreams, in the past, present and future.

It was unbearable, though they could not leave until they found the chest.

He needed to pull himself together, he thought.

He knew what would help.

He got his backpack ready and prepared to go to one of the ancient portal sites.

Maybe the magic within would hold the answers he sought.

He began to wonder if the blaze might not be right under his nose.

The poem brought you where you let it and the words began to blur in his mind.

Picking up the book *The Thrill of the Chase*, Kieran took off in his jeep towards the river.

Letting his mind drift through the poem,

"Begin it where warm waters halt," he thought, how clever.

The beginning was the ending and vice versa.

You mirrored it to itself, looking within your own reflection to see the map.

The last pieces were missing.

He thought it had to do with the necklace in his dreams and the one in the chest.

He thought it was an energetic portal that rested both inside the chest and somewhere in the current dimension.

He was growing frustrated with the person who seemed to be ahead.

He decided to roam around town and see what he could come up with.

He needed to take his mind off of Rain and wanted to work through a couple clues.

He thought he had overheard something about a cavern on some folk's land that supposedly held artifacts.

People were not sure if the new landowners knew it was there and were not going to tell them.

It was rumored that this was an exit to the extensive underground caverns.

He was starting to hear about an ancient dragon, thought to be the mother of all dragons.

It was told that the dragon rested in Flathead Lake and waited for the right bloodline to arrive to awaken from a sleeping potion placed to protect her and the magic she contained.

He was curious what Rain was doing back here.

He thought she had said she would never return.

He briefly remembered her sharing about overhearing a serious discussion about herself and how it had frightened her.

They had been arguing that she was spoken of in prophecies, but it was doubted that she could rise to the challenge.

They had sent her to Spring Creek not long after.

He knew that the experiences there had scarred her deeply.

She was very quiet, but the rage simmered just below the surface and came out in tightly clipped sentences, when spoken of.

She had yet to let go of this.

It was one of the things that he had been annoyed by.

He did not understand why a person could not let things go.

Then, he had grown up pampered in a family of loving and famous people.

His childhood had been filled with adventures and easy living.

He was blessed with an extremely quick mind, sharp humor and a beautiful physique.

He had too much to think about.

He really needed to find out how to get in this cavern that the clues led to.

He had been there but could not find out how the cavern opened.

He thought it had to do with a dance and some stones.

This is as far has he had gotten, except in dreams.

He had been in the cavern, in his dreams.

The dreams were haunting him again.

CHAPTER XXV

AZTLAN

"The space between fact and fiction is often blurred by
the passage of time."

Forrest Fenn
The Thrill of the Chase

Sarah insisted they stop for breakfast that morning.

Something was wrong with Kieran's stomach.

It had the same sensation he felt when he was around someone from his past.

Someone he had not told his wife about.

Besides, after meeting Sarah, they had moved to New Mexico, together, for all it offered.

He thought the distance would have helped, he had not dreamt about her in at least a year.

He let the thoughts slide and pressed the anxious knot away, hurrying Sarah.

They had found an extremely likely spot for the box, and were on their way to get it.

He hoped.

When they reached the encampment that had hosted the travelers on the Oregon Trail, it lined up beautifully with the poem. There was even a dry Fenn Creek.

Braving the bear laden woods, they reached the bare hill, below the blaze.

The spot they had seen several days before looked disturbed, and he could see some kind of scuffle had happened.

He bent down and found an empty bullet shell, the past was telling a story loudly.

He did not trust what he felt, and began to move aside the dirt.

Several feet in, he realized if something had been there, it was gone.

He took a moment to drink in the delicious view, but only a short one, he felt uneasy here, and told Sarah they should just go.

He was irritated.

The dead ends were annoyingly deceptive in the enthusiastic assertions of thrilling clue interpretations.

Well, he was not one to give up, and figured he had just made a wrong turn and someone had beaten him here.

Seeing something glint in the dirt, he bent down and picked up the edge of some sparkly blue fabric and a bullet casing.

With annoyance, it dawned on him, whoever had beaten him here was female and was in danger.

The hunt was closing in and there were several searchers who meant business.

He pocketed one of the shells and the fabric, glanced around and he and Sarah made their way through the prickly sagebrush to the jeep.

Someone had been there, rooted around and left a general mess, throwing the glove box contents on the ground.

Most disturbing, all of his notes from the hunt were gone.

He gratefully saw that they didn't take *The Thrill of the Chase*.

There was a horseshoe sitting where the notes had been.

Sarah was anxious and looked frustrated.

She usually was a good sport, but it had been a long day and now someone had been by their camp and in their stuff, she was frazzled.

He decided to stick it out, as they had not found anything and it felt safe enough.

He checked the pistol under his seat, it was still there.

The only thing that still lingered in his mind was that he had extensive notes on his next spot to look.

Now someone would know where he was going.

Searchers had begun to figure out that there were multiple places that worked, and in these places, objects of power had been left, but someone was finding them first.

The poem was metaphysical and the Chroma, safe in a magical resting place.

The searching frenzy was at the height of its chaos with summer coming to a close.

Kieran thought they better hurry and pointed the car north, to Montana.

It was a race he intended to win.

He had information that nobody else had.

He dreamt of one of the entrance portals to Aztlan, and that the chest was the key inside.

He knew there were answers there.

The "Chroma" held the key to

places long ago, hidden, to protect their Power.

He was determined to find these answers and knew it was his destiny.

He dreamt of this, he dreamt of these hidden cities and lakes, Dragons flying peacefully, people cooperating and living in harmony.

It had been like this before it all was hidden when the first Serpentine ships arrived when Atlantis or Aztlan, as it is also known, was thriving.

The water had been warm.

They hid it below the Mountains, the lairs, the pyramids, the ancient Temples; the Mother Dragon was given a sleeping potion to last until awakened.

Begin it where warm waters end, yes, indeed, begin it there.

The landscape drifted by in glorious quiet as the motion of the car soothed his mind to a place of, at least, riotous calm.

CHAPTER XXVI

THE SOCIAL HOUR

"Are you polluting the world or cleaning it up...by cleaning your inner state you cease outer pollution."

Eckhart Tolle
The Power of Now

Chatter filled the lobby of the Syme's Hotel, every seat was filled with bodies of various shapes and sizes.

Christmas lights still hung, though the New Year had come.

Sarah wished Kieran would hurry back.

He had gone adventuring alone.

He needed some fresh air and was going to a site he had been to before. He had the secretive air that was annoyingly aristocratic, so she dared not ask more.

She was feeling alone and the people irritated her.

Someone was speaking Russian to his small boy, in rapid-fire tones that spoke of short temper and impatience.

An old dog panted by, his weight almost bending him over.

People trickled by at a steady stream, in various states of clothing.

Sarah was ready to leave this place, but Kieran was insistent they look here.

He thought he had found the Chroma, finally.

She thought it was probably just another dead end, but he seemed volatile lately and she was worried he would be more likely to think of more fun things if she complained.

She hated feeling like this.

She was starting to get depressed.

She had been prone to episodes of dark moods and despairing thoughts, but had not had a serious episode in years.

She felt the pull of the abyss of clawing despair reaching for her, though.

She loved him deeply but started to wonder if these secrets might be weighing her down too heavily.

Sarah watched as people were busy in their dramas, she had never felt so alone.

Deciding it was all she could handle, she rose, bumping into someone. "Excuse me," she stammered, looking up into green eyes laughing at her.

He was gorgeous, tall, with sandy hair. He winked at her and said in a thick Slavic accent, "No problem."

She felt much better after the flirty exchange and sauntered back to her cabin.

It was a mess, she picked up, and decided to call her Mom back, finally.

It rang a few times, and her Mom answered,

"Oh my God, there you are, I have been so worried."

Sarah dutifully filled her Mom in, but left out any part of trouble with Kieran. Her Mom did not like him, and would be delighted to hear she was worried. "Well, honey, you find that treasure, now, and you be sure to tell that no good louse of husband, dragging my daughter off to the middle of nowhere will not earn him points with me, unless y'all find it, then I get that bracelet, OK honey?"

Typical, she sighed.

Well, she pulled out the papers she had hidden and read some more.

Sarah began to sink into a feeling of dread as she read.

The history between the two would separate them, but time and time again, they had reunited.

She was not sure she would be able to pretend around him.

She shrunk farther into herself and began to obsess about how to get rid of Rain.

Sarah was pretty sure Kieran would not approve of the recent "work" she had been doing, and figured leaving this where he might find it would be a good idea.

How could she do it without implicating herself?

This was getting too complicated.

She felt herself slipping into a darker mood.

The phone interrupted her darkness, and she picked up, annoyed to be bothered from her plotting.

"Yeah?"

"Well, have I caught you at a bad time?"

It was time to pay her debt.

"So, I have a favor to ask of you."

"I need you to meet me in one hour, down Skunk Alley."

"OK."

Sarah had made a mess of it all, but guessed she better go see what this woman wanted.

There always was a price.

Last time, the information had cost her money and the delivery of a package, she felt funny taking it to the home she was directed to leave it at. She never knew what was in it, but had a feeling she did not want to.

She watched, from a distance, as the woman who answered the door opened it and then quickly fell to the floor.

Sarah had not stuck around to see if she had risen.

She gulped and dressed warmly.

It was freezing out there, and she hoped the clothing might hide her.

The people here were so nosy.

The gossip train ready to roll without coal.

She felt her face flush with resentment and embarrassment as she recalled coming around the corner to hear herself being discussed.

Someone had seen her flirt with the tall Ukrainian and was wondering if she had snuck into his room.

The nerve.

She was married to the love of her life and he was off chasing some stupid box, and obviously in love with Reagan Bauer.

How could they blame her for smiling at a cute man who flirted, and why should that mean she would cheat?

Did they not have anything better to do than discuss others?

When were they leaving?

She angrily wrapped her purple scarf, a bit too tight, and huffed out of the room.

She was terrified.

She dreaded each step toward the dark little Saab and the woman in it.

"Sarah, we appreciate you coming."

There were two of them.

The woman, Katherine and another, who threw a chill, but looked beautiful to the eye.

"Please take this vial. You will need to enter this home, and place it in the water jug, by the door."

The directions were to Rain's.

Sarah swallowed.

"Sure."

She bet they knew that hurting Rain, would not bother her.

Rain soaked in the private claw foot tubs until she was shriveled.

Then she filled the tub with more hot water, dunked under, blew out and remembered the first piece she had found by Hebgen Lake, Montana.

She thought it was a joke, or another hunter's tag.

It was in a small box and had rested under two, lined up blazes.

They had been below the big, obvious blaze, and Rain had almost missed the first one.

Had she not been there right at sunset she would have missed the second, too.

She had begun at the conjunction of the Firehole, Madison and Gibbon and gone down the canyon.

Going below the gate, and towards Hebgen Lake.

Just below the dam, at heavy loads and water high, there was an enormous white blaze on the rocks across the Madison.

She had crossed the swift and cold creek, climbing by where nine of Osborne Russell's men had fallen, through the woods.

When she reached the blaze.

She looked quickly down.

And then she kept looking.

It had to be around there somewhere.

She looked until the pink of the sky heralded a darker hue.

Then she saw it.

A horseshoe nailed to the middle of a cottonwood tree.

She got right up to it and puzzled, it was bronze.

There was something scratched at the bottom. She could hardly see the small "ff."

She had found it, but where was the box?

She began to dig, and just as the light was dropping over the hill, she caught the glint of something about nine feet away.

She needed a stretch so went over.

It was another horseshoe with an "ff."

This one was upside down.

When she reached up to feel it, it turned and a lever released a series of latches and springs and a small bronze box popped out.

It was an exact replica of the chest, inside was a tiny dragonfly.

She smiled and put it all in her pack.

She still had to get back across the creek, and on the other side, she had spotted signs of recent bear activity.

All the warning signs around about hungry, thieving bears, had her a touch worried to be out alone, at night, by the water, which masked any approach.

Someone was very clever, or Forrest was leaving other clues to figure out.

She was too tired to care.

Coming back to the present.

Rain hopped out of the tub, coated her skin in coconut and a few essential oils.

She was moving really fast.

She greedily gulped the single file aligned water, then remembered to slow down.

It tasted a bit bitter.

She was just excited.

She was on her way to New Mexico, to see Forrest.

He had agreed to meet her and had said he might take her to his ruins.

She put her clothes on still damp skin, and walked out into the lobby.

She felt a twinge of pain, but ignored it.

Sarah was there, and Rain did not appreciate the look she was sending her.

Sitting right next to Sarah, as a challenge, she unwound her long hair and sat by the fire to dry it.

Sarah scowled at her, looked almost guilty and Rain could see her swallowing something she wanted to say.

Rain pulled her energetic cloak around herself and hoped to bounce her back enough to avoid whatever conflict this woman had.

Rain was not about to open herself up.

Feeling her hair was dry enough, and hoping not to see Kieran, she bolted up and hurried into her VW.

As it sputtered to life, she saw Sarah come out, and Kieran was just pulling into the lot.

She gave him a halfhearted wave and drove out seeing him glance between the two women.

She wished he would leave, and intended to talk to him about it.

Her head started to pound and her fingertips got numb.

Her heart began to hammer in her chest.

She just made it home and got several drops of the medicine in before she fell onto the floor.

She awoke feeling better, but tired.

Her whole team had needed to work on her.

CHAPTER XXVII

FF

"To realize this truth you must live it... As the joy of being...
Then you can be free of time... Loss of now is loss of being...
It represents the most profound shift in consciousness... Are
you polluting the world or cleaning up the mess, as within so
without... Once you realize you have a choice, you have the
power to access the now."

Eckhart Tolle
The Power of Now

Forrest had invited her to visit him.

He offered to show her around, she was looking for the chest and had developed a curiosity and a fondness for him.

Rain knew she had to see into his eyes to know who he really was.

Rain could feel his energetic trails all over and felt his spirit of adventure lingering behind, in each place she knew he had been.

He had left objects, and since she had found them, they felt to be for her alone.

The drive was beautiful, except Salt Lake.

She hesitated to pass through, but wanted to see some people.

She had a client, an M.D., Jack, who begged her to stop.

Approaching the smog, she placed a mask on her face, and hoped for the best.

She needed travel money, so agreed.

It was hard to run from the chaos of the world, it reminded her of the urgency of the quest.

Turning down 3300 South, she pulled into her old office.

Jack was waiting in his silver Land Rover.

She smiled and waved, and he got out.

She enjoyed his tall and calm presence and he understood the deep energetic benefits of her work.

She laughed a bit when the gals at the salon upstairs glowered at her as she walked by.

They never had been polite.

But then they were not going to make $200 that hour and get smiled at, like Jack was smiling at her.

"I have missed you. I tried surfing Backpage, but was disgusted. I lucked out with you."

He said, hugging her in the privacy of her office.

"You too, handsome, how ya been?"

They bantered and started the session.

She had set the office up with candles, oils and had energetically cleansed it already.

The silk sheets and scarf felt smooth and cool contrasted to the portable fireplace and candles.

Rain breathed in and invited Jack to join her.

She opened his chakras, and ran her hands softly along his skin.

Noticing a new tattoo, a snake and stick, she thought how nice it was to have an M.D. understand ancient energy.

And how the attraction they felt for her got in the way of her own diagnosis.

Any type of M.D. she would go see had come to see her.

From the family guy, to the psychiatrist.

She knew what they were thinking.

And she really did not need their diagnosis or treatment.

The sickness and cure was within her power, she breathed this knowledge in gratefully.

She enjoyed inviting Jack into a timeless place, and reminded him he was perfect and made of love.

She felt the room shimmer, and fought her own sexual energy and needs and focused on him, sending him the energy building inside her.

She slowly peeled off layers of energy, clothing and boundaries of time and space, letting him float in senses and joy.

As the music wound down and the energy slowed to a sleepy place, she fought urges to think and allowed more being to occur.

She would be leaving soon enough.

Forrest was waiting for her.

She swallowed a few drops of oil and hoped that would take care of the blooming bug she felt.

She was getting tired of fighting so hard and thought this felt strange.

Knowing she was going to see the delicious landscapes again and that she was close to finding the treasure box gave her motivation to push forward.

She imagined a cloud of healing descend upon her and wash out this feeling.

The queen snorted in disgust.

"Who taught her that?"

"That potion was not supposed to be cleared out so easily."

"If Rain can disconnect from her feelings and thoughts, she will be able to bring the now into light."

"We cannot have her do this."

"Has anyone been able to penetrate Forrest or anyone close to him?"

"No, my Queen, he has a powerful spell of protection surrounding a large area and all of his family."

"He watches Rain, and helps her, we think he knows about her and the old prophecies, but he holds old relics from the arrival of our ships, lifetimes ago, that our enemies brought."

"How did these artifacts survive?"

"Just like the rest of it, my Queen, hidden, by those dirty little humans."

"With the stones and symbols, we cannot go close."

"He needs her to find it so he can pass on the magic within, but she has to find it, he cannot just give it to her, it was written to be a quest, we have found the old scrolls contained within the chest originally, and destroyed them as you wished, but you know the information is within each heart."

Usually not prone to losing control, the queen threw her glass of black brew against the wall of the ship and hissed for her servant to get out, she fumed and slithered about her chambers.

CHAPTER XXVIII

ROAD TRIPPING

"Carre-Shinob was an Aztec Temple containing
the treasure of Montezuma... Fate is often devoid
of reason... There can be no doubt that the sacred
relics of the Aztecs-ancestors to the Utes-were
returned from which the gold came from... Mine
was a blood oath, and it would be worth my life
to violate it. There is no treasure so valuable as
to be worth more than life itself... I will say only
that I felt a need to make such a record, to honor
the memory of those long forgotten, and to clarify
once and for all time the question of ownership...
It is the sacred treasure of the Utes, and to them
only does it belong."

Kerry Ross Boren, Lisa Lee Boren
The Gold of Carre-Shinob

Driving south on 191, she stopped at the Hole in the Wall and used the restroom.

She figured she would head towards the Ute Tribal Council tree near Grand Junction, Colorado.

She gathered some branches and let herself travel back in time, when they had sat around a younger version of the giant cottonwood and spoken of peace.

Some of the first women allowed to sit on council, sat around this tree.

One of them was her great Grandmother, where the seeing bowl had come from.

She had ancient magic and practiced it without shame.

It was only after the greed disease was instilled that the magic had to be hidden again.

It had been misused before, in Atlantean times, and the people had placed chips to suppress memories and magic until now.

It was awakening.

The branches rested on the dash with some other objects and she rolled towards Pagosa, or previously known as Navapachute.

An ancient Spring, and she was placing the magic already awakened within. As she traveled south, she was following an old pathway.

The Santa Fe Trail.

She stopped at Cow Canyon and walked where the pictographs pointed towards one of the Seven Sacred Caves.

She could feel the hardened brown feet trudging with their loads of gold, stolen, then stolen again.

They took load after load through these hills and hidden it from Cortes.

The most important mine held treasures, old and new.

The gold had been mined and worked there, and treasures from Montezuma's cache lay waiting.

Her people had been enslaved and forced to work until death in these mines.

When the Spanish invaders were kicked out, the Ute's took over the original mines again.

The weight of protecting these secrets was heavy and taken with the utmost serious blood oaths.

The unfortunate error had come with a dream instilled by Serpent influence. A vision was given that the secrets were to be given over to the first tall-hatted individual.

Unfortunately, this was Brigham Young, a Mormon and accused alchemist. The gold fever had been effectively spread.

The medicine of the Great Bear, originating in the great island home of Aztlan, and the Aztec roots of her people, waiting for the return of Quetzalcoatl, had been turned into a great shadow body feeding off of itself.

The alchemy of the gold misunderstood and coveted in the universe was causing great drama and a negative field.

Her relatives, cousins of the Colorado Ute's, the Timpanoga's or Laguna's together with the Southern Ute's had kept out invaders from various countries and brave treasure seekers.

Rain had to convince them, that the whole history was a farce.

The gold belonged to Gaia, and She needed it back.

Given the deep history, emotions attached and the rapidly growing disease of greed, the challenge needed magic to lift the fog.

She had made it to Santa Fe, taking a route supposedly closed for winter travel, she braved it, as the road looked good.

About half way there she regretted her decision, but turning back was not an option.

Gunning it through the deep sand and flooring it to make it up the windy snow laden curves, Rain hoped she would be on time to meet Forrest.

He was taking her to his San Lazaro ruins, and Rain could barely contain her excitement.

She was nervous.

Forrest was powerful, in a soft way.

He made her sweat with nerves.

So far, she had eight objects, and assumed there was a ninth.

Though the eighth piece, a small dragon, had been so hard to find, she wondered about the chest.

Forrest seemed surprised she had made it this far, and Rain thought she caught a hint of anxiety in his voice when she had told him about the dragon.

Forrest liked to know his searchers, and kept close tabs on all of them.

Rain did not know, one of the parties following her, Forrest had hired.

Forrest had cheated death already, but had such passion for the senses, he could not imagine leaving.

So, as much as he was entertained, he did not want it found, and thought he had made it so

hard, it would take thousands of years to find.

By then, if people were angry, it did not matter.

He was waiting for Rain to get there.

He thought he would never see the dragon he had so carefully hidden in the Sinks Canyon.

It was the second time Thermopolis had been used, as the warm waters halting the first just below the Boysen Dam, there were three tunnels.

The blazes had been in the **second tunnel.**

He had left a jade dragon there.

Forrest did things in twos, in honor of his Mom's twin.

The tiny blazes had been extremely hard to see, Forrest was impressed with this girl, and flattered at her obvious attraction to him.

He and Peggy laughed at Rain.

"Another obsessed hunter, Bubba?"

"Yes, this one is pretty smart. I am going to meet with her."

He gave his wife a long kiss, and ran his hands over her shoulders.

At 84, he was still in love with his high school sweetheart, Peggy.

She was a beautiful woman, and playfully grabbed his rear.

"I will see you when you get home."

She liked this search, it gave him spunk.

She had worried so much about him, and now he was so happy and vibrant.

Rain sat nervously waiting in the Collected Works bookstore.

The oversize, brown leather couch swallowed her and the people reading or waiting seemed brimming in contained anticipation.

A presentation about nuclear energy was about to begin.

The tension in the room was portentous.

City energy still had a way of working itself into her, and she felt the nerves of electronics and moods pulsing through her, vibrating at an annoyingly fast pace, making her sweat and shake.

She was nervous enough meeting Forrest.

Rain was not sure why he agreed to meet her, and take her to San Lazaro, he never did that.

He knew she had the dragon.

That must be why. She was close. This must be the final key.

He strode in, tall and confident, with a walk that still spoke of fighter pilot.

His blue eyes twinkled as he softly extended his hands.

"Rain, how are you? I hear you found something you want to show me? Can I buy you some coffee?"

"No, thank you, good to see you. Let's just go, I am nervous in here."

"OK, I can see that. You need to relax."

"I will, as soon as I am outside."

She grinned at him.

He flushed and turned away.

He had a way of bringing her emotions to the surface and she felt a certain lack of control over her response to him.

She needed fresh air, desperately.

She shivered and shook, tears close to the surface.

Most never noticed this, but Forrest did.

"Rain, you need to relax."

He said, again, feeling sorry for her.

He recognized anxiety from his own chewing on it.

"OK, Forrest, I will try, but I do much better outside of the city."

"Well, by all means, let's get out of here, then."

He gently grabbed her arm and led her out, Rain dutifully followed, noticing how subservient she felt around him.

He had strong magic.

She was not used to feeling confused by male energy.

She had practiced control for years and was puzzled, and slightly amused but worried by this.

He was always a gentleman, but Rain could feel the tension beneath.

They drove in his beige jeep, stopped at a feed store and had brunch.

Rain had her moment to observe him flustered after he had knocked the table getting up and spilled his milk.

She had seen it, but had hoped the waitress would have cleaned it by the time they got back.

He had asked her into the feed store to show her the peacocks they had, as she had admired them coming into the gravel parking lot.

The milk was still there and spread over the table, when they returned. Rain knew Forrest had a particularly sensitive personality to being singled out.

She quietly and quickly grabbed a rag, and as nonchalantly as possible, mopped it up, pretending she did not know what happened and not giving it undue attention.

This seemed to be all right and she sensed he liked how she handled it.

She turned to look at a brightly painted peacock.

He stuck the nanochip into her sandwich.

The next bite.

"I want to see the dragon you found, don't keep me waiting."

She pulled out the small Dragon, and gingerly handed it to Forrest.

"I did not think I would see this again, tell me, what does it mean to you?"

Rain was cautious in her reply, "I really do not know, yet."

She saw, from her side view, him shrug in resignation or disappointment.

"Well, let's go to the ruins then. I hope you know, this is special. I cannot take everyone out here, let's keep it quiet."

"Sure, Forrest, nobody knows we have met even."

Perfect, he thought.

She was the right one for finding the chest, if anybody was.

He was not sure he would get to witness this in his lifetime, nor was he so sure he wanted to.

The game was too much fun.

The consequences of it getting in the wrong hands, dire.

He watched as she struggled and hunted.

He did not have a hard time keeping a secret.

The military had taught him well.

Now she could not hide even within.

He was not the only one who knew where it was, but he protected his best friend from unwanted ha-rassment, by saying he was the only one who knew.

But then, they had kept a secret together for thirty years, it was not hard to add another.

Also, she did not know all she needed to.

Passing through several key coded gates, the dirt track got rougher and the jeep bounced.

When they stopped, there was a pile of archeological supplies, and many objects lined up and sorted.

Forrest wandered after giving Rain a gallon size Ziploc bag, telling her to collect what she wanted.

Rain felt the ground vibrating with softly moccasined feet, heard the clamor of camp.

She began to feel realities and time colliding.

It was not often that so many objects of power were left in one place.

The energy was still attached and the bustle of a city could be found under a thin veil of today.

She walked and knew she had been there lifetimes before.

They had abandoned this place.

A sickness had come.

Maybe this was where it started.

She hesitantly placed a few things in the bag, surprising Forrest with her choices.

The one true prize was what they called gaming pieces.

Rain knew they were old Runes.

Magic stones that held answers.

Here was one that had rested in her pouch lifetimes before.

It was round, with reddish tones and said

"IF."

Perhaps, if you will or can, find me and make the changes happen, it spoke to her, in a language she understood, the Old one.

It begged her to awaken and continue, reminding her she had made an oath to be here, now.

Forrest had to go home he said.

He had gotten annoyed it seemed, when she asked what was in the cave.

"It is just a clay mine."

Rain heard the line,

"Tarry scant with marvel gaze."

Echo in the wind.

Curious. This is not eight point two five miles north.

Something behind this was asking her to keep walking.

It called her.

Forrest started his jeep.

"Rain, my wife is sick, I need to get home, but if you will come down here, we can look by the creek. This is one of my favorite places here. I like to swim here in the Summer. Do you like swimming?"

"I do."

"You can swim here in the Spring, the water is nice."

He had taken her to the ruins and was inviting her again.

"No, way, you are so lucky to come here so much, are you serious, I can come back here?"

"Sure, Rain."

"Let's go." He said.

They packed up, crossed the still dry creek bed, climbed in the jeep, and headed North.

As they crossed through several gates again, Rain thought about that dry creek bed and the annoyed look Forrest had.

She began to get some ideas.

"So, Forrest, you come out here a bunch?"

"Yes, several times a week."

"It is my favorite place to be."

The favorite place stood out to her.

"Oh, I would love to be able to do that."

"You are lucky to own this."

"Why don't you come and camp this Spring?"

Her heart jumped.

"I would love to!"

She was so excited, she would come back as soon as she could. This place held such stories, and she wanted to know them. The stories felt to be just under a layer in her brain.

She needed to look at the book he wrote about the ruins and study more.

She had come for the pleasure and experience, these ruins were drawing her in.

She aimed to study them carefully and come back soon.

Forrest gave her *The Secrets of the San Lazaro Pueblo*, *Too Far to Walk*, *Seventeen Dollars a Square Inch*" and a huge hug.

"Rain, come back soon, I will miss you."

He thought she was interesting and stood a chance. Now, he would know where and who she was with all of the time.

If somebody was going to find it, he wanted to know.

He liked her, thought she might find it and do the right thing.

She would be back soon she promised, and thanked him for the beautifully signed books.

He was a talented writer.

She started flipping through *The Secrets of the San Lazaro Pueblo*.

It fell open to the page about the **Medicine Rock**.

This was a butterfly shaped rock that had been hand dug out to create a mystical ceremonial Power structure. A shaman would stand on top and tribal members would emerge from the tunnel, in front of the fire.

A huge blaze.

If you looked down, the **tunnel**, from above, an altar shelf lay hidden by a woody pack rat's nest.

Forrest said they left it, as "Some secrets are best left alone."

Rain puzzled.

What of the cavern in Montana?

Forrest said it was at least eight point two five miles North of Santa Fe. This was South.

Would he lie?

"Yes," thought Rain.

He would.

Or it was not a lie, just a play on words, he did this.

"Mirror, Mirror, on the wall!"

Rain started the drive back through the pastel melted landscape, through the red rock desert, across the flat sagebrush and back to the still brown, but snow capped mountains of Utah.

The whole way she could not stop thinking about this rock.

Medicine Rock.

She thought maybe the cavern up North was where it started, she needed to go in it.

She had the necklace she needed, but the distractions were so great, she just had not tried.

Well, that was about to change.

She was so wrapped up in Forrest, she was forgetting the true quest. This was not about treasure.

Realizing the duality within it, the twin nature of both the start and the end, she worked the poem.

Begin it where warm waters halt.

This would be where the glacier came through, she thought, starting at the cavern. She took it in the canyon down, too far to walk, because you went all the way to the Medicine Rock camp. The directions told you so, as this was the well-known blaze of the day. Heavy loads and water high was **Shiprock**, then be sure to bear left, or nigh.

Home of Brown could be literally be interpreted as the San Juan Pueblo. She knew now it was to the left of Shiprock, below the Pueblo. This placed her in New Mexico. She was looking for a blaze, which would be the one on Forrest's land. The ancient one, with history old and new. He went there three times a week.

There was a perfect place of power to entomb oneself.

He had found his treasures there, many of them.

He would leave the chest in his favorite place.

For the final pieces of the puzzle, since Forrest lived and had been tricky about the location, Rain had to get through him.

She had stopped, on her way home for a soak and water meditation in Lava, Idaho.

The new Watsu pool was delightful. Colored lights surrounded pleasant owl and vase fountains, the creek rushed by, singing soothing tunes.

Rain floated on her back admiring the drifting shapes in the sky.

She felt weightless and exhaled all of her tension from the trip.

The water temperature was perfect, it felt silky and smooth.

The minerals made her feel soft.

The nagging pain in her lower left side vanished.

This one spot still lingered, and seemed to resist the medication.

The waters were key for soaking into it.

She sighed and hummed.

A giant hawk soared over, dipping low enough she could see her eyes. They stared at her.

She heard,

"Little Sister, you must continue to fight and do what is right, the answer lies in both the dark and Light."

The hawk whistled, circled four times then glided off gracefully, dipping in the wind, here and there.

She needed to figure out how to get back, as soon as possible. She was pretty sure Forrest did not intend for her to find the chest, as she now knew much more about him.

She sensed she would struggle on multiple levels to get it, though she knew where it rested.

Perhaps the answers were by the pictographs.

She better get home.

In response, her amulet stirred.

She packed everything, said goodbye to the owner, loaded Dasher, and ran back in for hot water.

Leaving Lava, Rain realized she had opened up that predatory energy by even speaking to clients.

She had been getting requests for appointments from numbers that should not be able to find her.

The owner of the Inn, had overheard her talking about Hot Springs, Montana.

He said he had a friend up there, but she had changed her name because of legal trouble.

Did she know Iris?

Rain swallowed a desire to share more, but said,

"She asked me for a ride to Salt Lake."

"Don't do that unless you want to go to jail. They are after her."

As Rain was leaving, with her hot water, she saw a police officer talking to the desk clerk and owner.

There was a reward for "Iris" and information leading to her arrest.

Rain had a feeling she better stay out of this, but already was in it.

A standard issue, black Ford was on her tail.

She thought about how she could lose the leech and sighed.

It had been nice to have this factor gone for a while.

They did not follow her in Montana.

She only had to worry about aliens and other treasure hunters for a while. These guys were back.

How did they know where she was?

She had not advertised and only had spoken to a few people.

It dawned on her.

Andy was jealous she was meeting Forrest again.

Forrest had ignored him, even though his story was interesting.

Maybe Forrest knew who he really was behind his cover of financial guru and amateur archeologist.

Andy had sent them after her.

How could he?

But then he said his wife was having a really hard time with his job.

He saw up to three body rub specialists daily, and claimed he never got turned on.

Rain knew the truth.

He already had mistresses and was sure he was seeing another suspect, outside of his cover.

He had shown up in her grey sporty car and had lied about who it belonged to.

Rain had seen her later, and had not been able to decide to be jealous or disgusted at him.

She had surprised herself, and though she had feelings for him, she just did not care.

The whole secretiveness of his job, hers, and their convoluted relationship had taught her much about herself.

The sex had been fantastic, some of the best ever.

The emotional price of loving a secret, too deep for it to work.

He taught her much about working for an undercover and deeply technological spy organization.

Specifically, how to get away and how one actually could evade the system.

She stopped and looked at the map.

The Ford pulled over not far from her.

Amateur or threatening, she would see soon enough.

It was one thing to follow and another to be so bold as to be obvious.

Rain had learned to smell them from afar and noticed when they followed. Even the good ones.

This guy obviously was just lost.

This was just her head playing tricks, this car turned off after awhile, when they drove again.

Rain thought she was losing it.

What had Forrest done to her?

She better hurry back and get focused.

She was pretty sure Andy did not care what she did anyway.

Maybe she was hoping he cared enough.

"Why should he? I was just his job. The rest a free bonus."

He had even said once,

"I can't believe I am getting all this for free."

She had just dressed up in black, high heeled, thigh high, Russian pirate boots and a fur trimmed, black velvet coat.

Nothing else.

He had screamed his orgasm.

The jab at the cost or not for the sex had stung.

She turned up the Reggae Dub Step and moved as much as she could while driving.

She was alive, looking at beautiful views, her dog beside her, his head out in the chilly air, right now, she was fine.

He backed off.

She had sensed him.

He had been watching her in the pools and was daydreaming about the lithe long legs when she had pulled over.

He had too, without thinking much.

She knew he was there.

He dropped way back, turned on the locator and just watched the bleep move.

The sagebrush gave way to forest and rolling hills as she neared Montana. She stopped for gas in Dillon, relieved to be back in her home state.

She liked the attitude of Montana.

Tough and leave you alone, but neighbors were just that.

A small town insulated and isolated, protected you in the folds of who was who or not.

She trusted the rawness of the hills, still suspicious of the advances of time, her chattering head felt held in the vast spaces filling her mind.

She made it to Hot Springs, and decided to head right to the pools.

Her suit was ready, so was she.

She pulled into Symes, and the first people she saw were Iris and what must be a client.

She saw Iris say something to him and then he looked at Rain like she was naked on a pole.

Rain did not appreciate this woman and needed to set things straight.

She had heard from the owner of Lava, enough to make sure she steered far away from her, whoever she was.

She was wanted by the law, and Rain knew for sure, it was a trap. Iris needed a way out of her trouble.

The energy Iris fed off was predatory and sexual, what Rain offered was different and pure love, despite the connotations.

Rain walked up, and threw a huge bubble around herself.

In false cheer,

"Hey there, Iris."

"This is Mark, the Senator I told you about. He really wants a four handed session."

"Pleased to meet you sir, I told Iris, already, I do not do the same kind of work, and am not seeing clients anymore, sorry to disappoint you."

She could feel the glare behind her back.

Iris was setting up a studio in town, and Rain knew that meant she was bringing dark energy to a place meant for real healing.

The senator would keep trying.

He wanted to get in touch with her, but was not sure how to do so without asking the older one he had been seeing.

She was OK, and always satisfied his needs, but he thought the fat belly and bikinis were a bit much.

She just could not give up the youth.

The young one was appealing.

He knew, once these women started this work, it was hard to resist.

He had spotted the quick assessing glance the beautiful, athletic and tall girl had sent him.

Her hair hung to her waist almost, and the bright bathing suit she wore conservative.

He could see the taught muscles in her long dancers legs, under the purple one piece.

Her biceps had a distinct cut and he fantasized about the rest of her.

"That little bitch. I am sorry."

"Not a worry."

He would be thinking of someone else when she did her massage later.

He closed his eyes and imagined Rain touching him.

Rain walked to the back pool to be alone and get the stare off her.

She better get organized to go to the pictographs, with the necklace, soon.

She had a few things to take care of first.

She ran home, grabbed some things, and sped back to town.

After what she had learned about Kieran and Sarah in New Mexico, her temper was flaring.

Rain had decided she would look around in their house.

She knew they were still in Montana.

She had become very skilled at getting in and out of places unnoticed.

She did not like to guess and was tired of wondering what they were doing there.

Kieran was hiding something, this she knew.

She did not find much in the tidy adobe.

She was surprised when a small grey cat came running out.

Kieran hated cats.

She nosed around opening cabinets, looking at photos, opening drawers. They each had an office, and each office held the secrets she knew had been there. Sarah's was harder to find.

She had hidden the paperwork well, but there it was.

Papers from a known black market adoption agency, recently exposed as having dark magic attached, in the web of underground information, fell out.

It was just speculation, but Sarah was in trouble dealing with these people. From the looks of it, Kieran had no idea.

Nothing had come of it.

Now, to his office.

She spent just a minute inhaling the wooly smell of him.

She could just see him leaning back in this chair she had sat in before. None of his furniture was new, he had gotten scores of valuable antiques from his wealthy family in Wyoming.

The desk, was an old French writing desk, with a secret chamber accessible with a few turns of a complicated lever system.

A whole compartment swung open.

He still had all of the things she had given him.

Everything was right there.

The pictures and birth and death certificate, a lock of hair.

Rain picked it up, smelled and thought she might die.

The crushing grief and guilt descended.

Katy had been dead long enough already, when they found her, there was nothing that could have been done.

If only she had not been so tired that night.

Katy had been sick for almost a month and alternatives were not working.

Rain had reluctantly admitted she needed something really strong for her infection, and consented to antibiotics everyone was pushing to give Katy.

As a baby, she just could not get anything herbal and strong enough to work.

Her lungs were filling and the fever had been steady for three days. Nothing would stay down.

Katy was withering, dehydrating.

Rain had fearfully given her a dose, watched, but fell into an exhausted sleep as Katy seemed to be resting, finally.

When she woke, Katy was gone.

The baby experienced a slower, deadly reaction, quietly stopping breathing, slipping away.

Rain felt a hot tear splatter on her arm, and realized she had been sitting there for a while.

Something caught her eye in the pile of stuff.

It took a moment to realize it was the top of the poem.

Rain pulled out a pile of notes and it dawned on her, Kieran was looking for her treasure.

She was furious and forgot the grief.

She angrily gathered up her things, left him a tiny note, and took all of his.

That was why they were in Hot Springs.

He thought the chest was there.

From the looks of his notes, he had been right behind her, the whole time.

She wondered if he knew.

CHAPTER XXIX

ROOTING

"Unless someone like you cares an awful lot,
nothing is going to get better, it's not"

Dr. Seuss
The Lorax

She pulled angrily into the lot, barely missing a car, as hers slid on the ice. Rain was furious and trying to control the feelings of guilt, grief and rage. How dare he still be here.

How dare he look for her box.

Never mind Forrest had left it for anyone to find, Kieran should leave her quest alone.

Sarah was in the lobby and looked surprised to see her.

Well, Rain was done playing nice and sauntered over to Sarah.

"Hey there, I was hoping to talk to Kieran for a minute, is he around?"

Sarah looked horrified, like she was not going share, when Rain sent her a dominant glare.

"I think he is back in the cabin."

"Thank you, it will not take long. I can ask you too, when are you leaving?"

"Well, I am not sure, he is still working at that dig site."

Rain's jaw tightened, she hated being lied to.

"All right then, I won't take too much of his time."

She expected Sarah to be on her heels any minute, so hurried back to the small cabin they had moved into after the first week in the hotel.

Cabin 9 was back in the corner of the lot, away from the main hotel and other cabins.

She knocked and he answered, having just showered.

He looked startled for a second, and then pleased.

They reunited once, just like this.

He seemed to remember himself and put on a different guarded smile.

"Can I come in, or should I wait?"

"Come in."

"Good to see you, we have not talked much."

"Look, I want to know why you are looking for the box?"

He stared for a second.

"What box?"

"Yeah, that is what I thought, anyway, it is not here. It was only another clue."

"Bullshit, you know about the cavern too. Did you open it?"

"No."

Now it was her time to lie.

She was done with him.

She decided it was time to move on.

Rain decided to call Cameron as soon as this conversation was finished and get moving with the chase.

Just as she was leaving, Sarah walked up.

She looked irritated and then shocked when Kieran was still in his towel. Sarah flushed, turning her head away from them.

Rain figured it best to clear out and booked across the lot.

It was good she left, Sarah let loose on him, she could hear it from the lobby, almost.

"Why didn't you get dressed! You should not have told her, tell me now about the two of you, you liar!"

It kept going.

Rain needed focus with clarity, so she headed to hike up the hill, this would help clear her head.

She realized she needed to stay in the present moment and not allow thoughts and emotions to take over and feed the disease and fog, walking would help.

Clearing this out and staying in moments of awareness was hard when the grief choked her, her rage as they chased her dream, the jealousy of their togetherness and her choked loneliness threatened to unleash a big shadow.

Rain gulped in the fresh air, as the vice grip closed in around her lungs.

Heat pressed into her heart, she felt the sweat start.

She started a technique she learned for clearing and cleansing energy and she walked faster.

Rain walked until she felt calm.

She knew Cameron was staying at Alameda's, so when she was done walking she headed over to his room.

A skinny, washed out, girl with missing teeth opened the door.

Her eyes were shifty and her energy zingy.

Cameron had been honest he was seeing other women, this woman puzzled Rain.

Well, she figured she better just head home, but just then he came out of the shower.

Great another half naked man, she did not want.

"Hey, Rain, this is Vanessa my friend I told you about, I was hoping you two would meet." He said glancing between the women in an obviously suggestive way.

"I need to get going, Cameron, you two have a fun time now."

She swallowed the disgust at herself, and knew she had been played, but she had at least enjoyed it.

He had a new assignment, Vanessa needed him.

She went home and started a course of full spectrum cleansing, and vowed to herself to stay focused, and not give into needs like this.

She felt set back and a bit bruised, certainly a sense of stupidity.

She needed to focus and find a good time to get to the cavern again to remember.

Right now, she did not feel good, though, and she felt the dark nipping her heels.

She called for Dasher, and did not think much when he did not come right away.

After thirty minutes, he still had not shown up.

She started to follow his prints, about 200 yards behind the shed, she saw the human prints, tire tracks, his prints, and blood.

Not just a little blood, but a bunch.

Oh, no, she hurriedly followed the path, and found him.

He was gone.

She gasped a choked scream and fell onto his heaped and bloody body.

He had been cut, deeply and crudely.

It had taken this long to bleed out, she could have saved him.

She ran back to figure out who had done this and why.

"Perfect, Katherine, that was a great way for Sarah to pay us back."

Shakira laughed and laughed more, she put out a general page that a new drama in Hot Springs, one of the most closely watched towns, with a key player, was happening.

The Serpents lined up and gathered energy off of Rain's pain.

Sarah drove away, horrified and shaking.

She could hardly believe she had put a knife in that poor creature.

But seeing the two together had given her the courage.

The look in his eyes had scared her, so she had plunged the special knife Katherine had given her, right where they said.

She thought, but then the poor dog had gotten away and limped off.

She had seen him fall, so she figured she had done the job right.

She had not, but the knife had poison in it as well, and it was a poison made to kill the special guardians of the Light Warriors.

Katherine had made sure there was enough poison to kill several of these special creatures.

Sarah had been told this act would put her even, and to not worry about her debt, if she could do this.

And the fact these people were after Rain, had her pleased.

Kieran had not reacted the way she planned when she had shown him the papers about Rain.

He had been furious at her jealousy, and seemed to have sympathy for the woman having whored herself out.

Things were not going well for Sarah.

She was considering just leaving and going home.

She was losing hope that her marriage would work out, and was competitive enough to want to be the one to call it.

She needed to calm down first, and get this blood off of her, and ditch the knife into the river, as instructed.

Sarah tossed it in, but she did not see the black cloud it spread when hitting the water.

She would not see this, as she was living it.

The darkness spread and a heavy air descended upon the peaceful valley. Arguments erupted and tempers became short.

The day felt long with suffering and disagreements.

Ruthie, who had been there for thirty years, waiting for the right time to banish the dark, felt the shift.

She looked into her seeing glass and saw a poisoned knife being tossed into the river.

She mentally erased the picture, and let the cloud be a cheerful one.

The Sun shot rays through the clouds and the moods lifted, most people unaware of the work being done to hold the space for them.

Ruthie curled back into her chair, with a cup of lemon mint tea and sighed. Keeping up with this was tiring her, and she was ready for the next Holder to arrive.

She wrapped her tie-dyed blanket tightly around her toes and leaned back in her chair.

She fell into a deep and dreamless sleep and this charged up her system, ready for the next round.

She would keep going until the very end.

Rain heaved the limp body of her dog over her shoulders and somehow made it to the tipi.

She wrapped him in her favorite blanket, got a fire going, and kept a blank expression.

When the fire was hot enough, she put his body, in the blanket her Grandmother had given her, and placed it on the fire and she watched it burn.

She felt a sinking fear, and walked into her tipi to smudge.

He had protected her and been her only real friend on some levels.

She realized she had been making mistakes and the cost was going to be heartbreaking.

She fell into a staring trance and just rocked by her fire, the tears spilling and splattering loudly, in the lonely solitude of her grief.

The sky darkened into night, Rain walked into the cold air, her boots crunching on the snow.

She looked at the stars and tried to feel the connection to the Universe. What she felt was shattered and beaten.

A dark weight fell onto her and she could feel the deep desire to run and hide from the pain and her desire for revenge.

She had been alone for a long time, but really felt it this minute.

The cold air, the styrofoam snow and the bright stars did nothing to penetrate the cloud.

She was in trouble, so was Gaia, if her mood stayed dark.

Sarah came into the cabin, she was shaking and had some blood on her.

"What on Earth?"

"Are you OK? What happened?"

"I hit a deer, it was horrible," she wailed.

He gathered her and held her as she sobbed.

He could not see her face, which was a look of delight.

She hoped that he would keep holding her.

He had been so cold since she had shown him the papers on Rain.

She nestled in and stopped crying, as it was just a deer, she did not want him wondering.

About an hour later, there was a loud knock.

When she answered, Rain stood, with a wild and dominant look, she pushed past Sarah, knocking her into the wall.

"Now, you wait a minute, you crazy whore."

"You, listen to me, I know what you did, and you will not go unpunished."

Sarah paled and stammered, whereby Rain pulled her Seeing Bowl out and showed Sarah the picture, which showed her stabbing Dasher with the otherworldly knife. Kieran walked in just then to see his true love and wife poised in such tension it struck time for a second.

Rain had long before learned to control her strength, but she had always had a time with temper. Hers was close to spilling past returning.

Seeing Kieran softened her, she loosened her grip on Sarah. She did not want to hurt the woman, for real, but if she saw her again, she would. She wordlessly showed him the killing scene in the Seeing Bowl, and looked at him in challenge. She would let him deal with this mess.

She saw some papers on the table, and figured while she was not completely logical, she would just go for it. She grabbed them and started reading. She had thought maybe they were related to the chest, but felt the wave of sickness fall into her heart.

Hers and his story, her struggles and then the year she had worked as a body rub specialist met her page by horrifying page.

Her eyes rose to meet his and stayed on them as the story reflected. She saw his sympathy and love. The relief flooded and she turned and strode out as quickly as she had come in. Tossing it all on the floor.

"You better pack, Sarah," Kieran said.

She hung her head and tried to catch his eye.

He was already gone.

Rain had never felt so low. In all the years of struggle, she always had some hope. Hers was fading, the ship was delighted and the serpents lined up to watch, throwing negative thoughts her way. She started to feel the stream of negativity and for a moment took a ride.

"You cannot do anything, there is no point to you, you need to kill yourself. You have nothing, nobody, no point, no purpose. Find a gun, do it fast. Hurry you worthless slut. Nobody is there for you, you cannot do this, who do you think you are?"

The thoughts streamed in.

She hung her head and cried as she slowly put one foot in front of the other. At least she could get home first.

She heard someone approaching and did not even care to turn her head. Let them take me, she lamented.

When he reached her, the look she had, scared him. It was the same one she had when they buried Katy, but worse.

He feared for her. She was not looking approachable, but he did not care. He could hardly process what he had seen, but he knew he still loved her, and was not going to let her just walk away this time.

The only thing that mattered was reaching her, before she retreated fully into herself.

Everything was coming full circle, and he was not letting her go this time. He knew how much he had let her down and how much he had hurt her, but he had seen the fire, though she had tried to hide it.

They could find the chest together. He was so excited to open his heart to her again, he neglected to think maybe she would not accept it.

She stared blankly at him.

"What do you want? Have you not ruined enough for me?"

He just kept looking at her, and sent waves of love.

He could see her struggling to stay in the dark thoughts, as the love pierced in.

Her head rose and it broke his heart to see the pain reflected.

"He was all I had, he kept me safe."

She looked uncharacteristically frightened and small.

He felt pulled to hold her, and he approached slowly and carefully.

Inching closer, he placed his hand on hers.

She jumped and withdrew, glaring at him angrily.

"Go home to your wife."

"She is leaving, I am done with her. I cannot even begin to say how sorry I am."

"I know you are, and if you touch me again, I will take you down."

He laughed, which was a mistake, and knew it before he hit the ground, her fists pummeling him.

His surprise lasted just a moment, as he realized she was really hurting him.

She was in a state of raw loss of control, and he was taking it.

It did not last long, as the thud of his body and the pain of hitting him woke her from her rage.

She sobbed and rolled off, huddled in a ball, ashamed already.

He risked it and moved in, grabbing her in a tight hold.

He held her tightly until he felt her relax.

She had always been like that.

Once heightened in an emotional state, light touch was enraging, she had to be held tightly and very still, or she would freak out.

He waited until she stopped shaking and loosened her muscles before releasing his grip.

He could tell she had softened enough and he dared to try and look in her eyes.

They were still clouded but clearing, and he could see the confusion and struggle at seeing him.

She would not remember much about flying at him, which he knew was good.

He realized she had been pushed way too far.

He hoped he could help.

She still was his heart and soul and he had never quit loving her.

He had a nagging feeling that this story was already preordained and they had planned it like this, but stayed in the moment with her, trying to bring her all the way back.

He softly placed his hands above her head and rested them there.

He let her drift into a sleep, he knew it would not last long, but would help her reintegrate into now.

He watched her rest, and looked around her space, fascinated with the way she had changed and dropped into her Native roots. Medicine bundles hung, with dreamcatchers, Eagle feathers, and strange looking herbs and roots hung everywhere.

He noticed her Altar shelf and walked closer.

He was surprised to see the tiny, Ming perfume vase resting in the center. He had given her the small, black, flowered vase with the tiny scooper.

It had held drops of some of the oldest Jasmine known to exist.

He picked it up, ignoring common boundaries with Altar spaces, as it had been in his family for centuries, and smelled it.

The vase still had the intoxicating fragrance that drifted pleasantly past the olfactory nerves straight to the brain and demanded attention in the loins.

He felt his tighten, as the memories of their scented nights together flooded in with the Jasmine.

He sat back and let the memories flow.

They were at his small cabin, out Gold Creek Road, in Sandpoint, Idaho. They had just met near Hot Springs, and had hit it off, more than well. He had invited her to his sacred retreat in the cedars and bracken ferns, quiet and spring fed, twenty acres of paradise.

They were young and still experimenting with life and he was still exploring his sensual side, and he appreciated beauty and women fully. He was not ready for the strong feeling he already felt for this woman, but figured he would enjoy it, for a while. He did not realize, then, that she was the one he was looking for so long.

They played and walked, running naked and wild, laughing and loving fully, without boundaries.

One, warm, but snowy day, they took some psychedelic mushrooms and wandered the property. As the mushrooms peaked in the trip, they began to speak different languages together, and faces from past lifetimes flashed before them, shifting shapes, ages, sexes, times, places and names but always together.

They performed a ceremony of marriage that was witnessed and celebrated by all of the creatures in the forest.

When twin flames united, it was always powerful.

Boundaries of time and space shattered and the love shimmered and grew, feeding the Light.

He flashed then, to them burying their daughter, and he felt the walls rise, but pushed them back.

He had to stay with her.

He was going to save her this time.

He watched her, until her eyes opened.

He could see the confusion, then pain and confusion again at his presence. He put his fingers to his lips and kissed hers.

She fought it for a second, letting thoughts collide with desire, then gave in. She felt the explosion of light before she saw it, and cried and cried as he kissed her tears and let the ecstasy of his touch wash over her.

Time faded into day again and she woke feeling rested and content.

She rolled over and looked for Dasher.

Then she remembered.

He was gone.

So was Kieran. Kieran ran.

He ran fast from the feelings.

He wanted the chest.

Rain had disrupted his life again.

He could not swallow the lump, it spilled as he threw a small bag, his backpack, *The Thrill* and what food he found in the half fridge into the jeep.

He loved her painfully.

Sarah had cleared out, leaving a mess.

Kieran ran his hands through his thick blonde, wavy hair, pulling and groaning.

He settled with Kara at the desk.

Martin stopped him and wanted to chat.

"Hey, man, you going to soak?"

"No, gotta go, headed home."

"Yeah, that is New Mexico, right?"

"Yep, hey, I will catch you next time, I need to hit the road."

"OK, bro, take care, later."

Martin wandered off with his big plastic basket he kept his soaking things in.

Kieran quickly left the lobby, not looking at the group gathered in front, smoking.

He did not want to get caught up again.

Peeling out of town, he regretted the pain he was going to bring Rain, but Together, this was their story.

CHAPTER XXX

SOLITUDE

"By the beginning of nineteenth century, one long-
standing myth of the West was the belief that
Europeans had arrived there before Columbus and
had started a race of "white indians." They number
eight hundred in all... Their dwellings are spacious
apartments nicely excavated in the hill-sides, and
are frequently cut in the solid rock... They subsist
by agriculture... pin and weave, and manufacture
butter and cheese... On the appearance of an enemy,
they immediately retreat to mountain caverns...
Barricading the entrance, they are at once secure
without a resort to arms."

*A Rendezvous Reader: Tall, Tangled and True Tales
of the Mountain Men, 1805 - 1850*

The loneliness that set in was familiar.

She needed to be alone.

Rain spent most of her life so.

Her world was lonely, but comfortable for her.

She had gotten comfortable with solitude on the "solo" part of her survival course at Spring Creek.

She had sat for almost five days in one spot, without talking to anyone. They wordlessly checked on the kids once a day, but if you had food, fire or water, it was up to you.

The first two nights she had not had fire and not much food.

They had been instructed to stay in one spot.

Those two nights had been extremely cold, frightening and the lonely in her head took her to quiet places inside.

The third day, the counselor who stopped by, kindly said "Hi" and left a metal match.

That was the best fire and words ever and she never let it go out, the rest of the time.

Hunger and the quiet, instructions to stay put, brought visions.

She dreamed deeply by her fire of enormous snakes and of a rattlesnake that bit her in the navel.

She spoke to the trees and let the fire soothe her.

She traveled to a land in the past.

They lived on low hills, in stone structures built and carefully aligned with the stars.

They had cows, goats and horses and were a peaceful people.

They ran and hid when trouble arose and had done so in New Mexico centuries before, leaving most of their possessions behind.

There were a few important pieces that nobody had gotten a chance to grab while under the attack of cannon balls.

One item was so important, a runner had been sent back to get it, but could not find it under the debris left in the South wing of the building.

It had been buried in an earthen box in the corner keeper hold.

The box contained a stone with unknown powers.

It had been found on the strange creature that they had discovered beyond their peaceful home.

This giant serpent-being had legs and a head with a face almost human.

The thing stole a bag of the metal they used in ritual.

The metal gifted from the Dragons, gold.

It was considered sacred medicine.

The safeguards and invisible barriers had killed the thief, but it was known now the stories were true.

An Oracle had spoken of a threat, and the people must hide all of the magic and protect the planet.

This battle was to go on for lifetimes.

The stone had been found on the alien.

The Council had been unsure what to do with it, when they had been attacked.

The stone was buried.

Forgotten.

Rain listened to the storm hitting the canvas of her tipi and decided she was leaving town, and packed her quick go bag. The car was always packed, to an extent.

The wind was bending and flapping, bearing down without mercy.

She was ready.

She was done with this place, felt so heavy and dejected and she let the weight wash over her.

She and Kieran had fallen together again many times, but leaving without a word was more than she could take, especially this day. She searched the bag where she had left her keys, they were gone.

She flipped every pocket inside out, and dumped the contents on the floor. No keys.

She searched, looked all around on the ground, peered inside the locked car, searched more, but they were not to be found.

She felt her heart speed up and her breathing got harder and faster, the sweat started, then the feelings. She felt the falling coming.

She needed out of there.

She did not feel safe.

She needed to get to the pictographs, then South.

She better walk.

She took her stick out.

It was of light wood and had carvings of her favorite animals on the staff.

The handle concealed a long, thin blade meant for skinning or slicing when needed.

She felt safer knowing it was there.

She slowed her breathing and began walking and she let the rain fall on her face. The cold spatters began to pull her from inside and she felt instead of panic, pain.

Pain, she knew.

Panic was new, since she had lived in Salt Lake.

The panic was the most uncomfortable sickly, sticky, sweaty mess she had ever encountered.

Once that wave started washing, letting it chew you on the bottom, then spit you out the other end, it was all she knew how to do.

The air and rain kept this attack mild, and she began to enjoy the movement.

She was passing by a house that had lights and music, lots of people wearing festive clothes.

It looked fun.

She longingly looked in the window for a while.

Stacy, the pretty, classy, southern girl, who worked at the hotel was hosting this.

Rain remembered seeing the flyers for the Fat Tuesday party, and felt her stomach rumble when the smell of Cajun gumbo wafted past her nose.

She had technically been invited, she thought, as it was an open party. She tended to make people nervous, especially when her feelings were elevated and she saw a man in there she preferred not to talk to.

He had been extremely rude to her at the pools.

Rain had seen him with Iris several times and figured she had gotten to him.

She had just looked under his garbage sack to see if she might stick her towel there.

She did not see possessions in a proprietary way, and meant no harm to his stuff.

He had yelled,

"Don't touch my stuff, stay away from me, you are crazy."

"OK, Marvin, not a big deal."

She was at the other side of the pools, and vowed to stay away from Symes for a while.

People were really getting into the shadow sides of themselves and were behaving in such a way that had Rain wondering who she could trust.

Despite the presence of social awkwardness and general mistrust, Rain stepped in.

Conversations dulled and the blues blaring did not cover the awkward energy that arose when she stepped in.

Well, she was hungry and did not care what they thought.

"It is not my stuff," she thought to herself and visualized a cloak of purple covering her.

She smiled and noticed an older gentleman across the room, near the food. Perfect, she headed his way and saw his face light up at the sight of her.

A friendly one.

He was a writer who was of the hiding bunch, but not from the law.

He was adorable to Rain, and had a soft strength to him.

He was writing about how hippies got made.

"Hey there, I thought I would not know anyone, you were at the pools yesterday, right?"

"Yes, we talked about your book, you got in the cold pool, I was impressed."

"I am glad you are here, I usually skip the party scene."

She filled her plate, declined a hurricane, and indulged instead in sparkling cider.

Her diet was strict, and this was enough of a deviance.

It was Fat Tuesday though, and the piled food felt comforting.

She and the writer bantered while she enjoyed the food.

A woman dressed in a very short, colorful mini, high boots, beads piled, sporting a feather hat approached.

"Hey, did you know Stacy is a famous cooking show host? She is here hiding from her fame."

Nothing surprised Rain.

"Sweet."

The blank look had her puzzled.

"Well, I have not watched TV in years, so would not know."

The woman just walked off.

Another woman who had been standing right there, began a high cackling laugh.

She just laughed and laughed.

Rain felt the tears rise and did not understand the joke.

"I have not watched TV," she said.

Continuing to cackle, she then started in on how the planet was being taken over by an alien race and everyone was possessed.

She made sense for a second then her sentences would trail off.

She was writing a book.

She said she was channeling it.

It was about a Serpentine Race stealing the planet.

The woman's eyes cleared and met Rain's for a frozen minute.

She spoke low and deeply, Rain strained to hear.

"It is time."

"What?"

The woman had vanished.

Rain finished her plate, and went to find the hostess.

"Thanks for everything."

"Well, I am glad ya'll came."

Stacy floated off in her purple dress and Mardi Gras crown, a tall hurricane teetering in one hand and a plate piled in the other, she air kissed and vanished into the growing crowd.

Rain began walking home.

She did not feel much better and wanted to know where her keys had vanished to.

She felt panic rising, then pushed it down, knowing she must need to be still.

She would find the keys when she needed.

A loud, rusty, burnt orange Prelude was approaching slowly.

She tried to see who was driving, but could not see the person under the small Stetson.

He had long grey hair, tucked under the hat in a braid.

He looked native.

No he looked like a cowboy.

Then the car pulled alongside her, slowed more.

The window was down.

Rain could see the sage and sweetgrass on the dash and she smelled the marijuana that was wafting out.

He smiled a huge grin.

"What is a pretty lady doing out here all alone?"

The question put her on guard, he noticed.

"Ya'll want a puff? I was fixin' to fire up a fatty."

Rain softened at the twang and looked deeply into his eyes before answering,

"Sure, my place is round the bend."

She felt like letting go entirely, the weed would help, and he seemed interesting.

Rain liked people who presented a challenging outward appearance to label.

This fellow was a walking contradiction.

He wore a cammo shirt, cowboy hat, a giant crystal around his neck, worn out Levis and outfitting boots.

"Hop in, sorry bout the mess."

The car was filthy. Rain thought hers was gross, this topped it. She relaxed as she noticed all the art inside his little Honda.

"You all right?"

"Sure, it is just down, on the left, under the H mountain."

"Yes, Ma'am, I know the spot, I wondered who was out there."

"My name is, Iam."

"Nice to meet you, Ian."

"No, Ma'am, Iam."

"Oh, OK, I am Rain."

"Stop right here, it is too muddy right now with all the snow melting, I almost got stuck and had to mud-bog it out."

He laughed deeply, and looked at her appreciatively.

"Ya'll been mud-bogging?"

Rain laughed.

"I spent some time in Asheville, North Carolina."

She had studied under a TIA Master and had been to several Tantric workshops.

She also had worked at Mission hospital.

For a moment, she let herself remember the feelings.

The hallway was empty, she needed help moving a heavy patient who had just had what was laughingly called a "Code Brown."

Nobody was around to help her.

She was hungry, had not eaten during her twelve hours, needed the bathroom, was behind in her documentation, medications, someone was being discharged early, and another needed two more IV lines started, STAT.

She started sweating and shaking, breathing fast, her back fired a pain message.

Then she looked where she was, still in a funky smelling and looking car, with an older man, she just met.

"Here it is, welcome."

They entered her tipi and he got out a pouch and a huge jar. When he opened it, the smell that came out had Rain giddy already.

She inhaled deeply and exhaled a spicy, yet fruity cloud of smoke.

She felt it almost immediately, but dared take two more hits.

She was rocked and fell back into his stories he was animatedly sharing. Rain enjoyed his loud twang, it filled her small space, and eased her aching heart.

Her loins were still aching from Kieran, her heart felt shattered.

This was helping.

This guy was funny.

Just then, Rain remembered a dream that a photographer had told her about. She was, or someone who looked like her, to find the chest, together with an older gentleman, of Southern descent.

"Hey, you ever been to New Mexico?"

"No, Ma'am, but I have always wanted to get to Chaco."

"What you think of treasure?"

"Not much, Ma'am."

Rain grinned, and told him the story.

He finished describing the golden, clawed necklace, in the box, without being told about it.

His connection was ancient.

"I just know that there's something there. The person who puts it on c'ain't bring harm, just good. I done thank I am supposed to help you."

Rain laughed, but felt the reality.

She had been looking alone, but the dreams spoke of two people finding it.

"Well, I was going to leave as soon as I find my keys, you want to go?"

"I reckon I got to."

She rooted around nervously and decided to check the bag again.

The keys were in there, along with a lollipop.

She long ago gave up challenging will like this, and just laughed.

"Right on, the keys are back from the void."

"I am ready to go, why don't you go get packed and come back first thing in the morning."

"All right."

"Pack light, for the desert and for checking out a snaky spot. I have a tent and everything, but not much room in my car. Bring food you like, a sleeping bag and some of that rocking herb."

She laughed, hugged her new friend and finished her preparations.

She halfway expected him to not show, but he was there first thing, with a couple of packs and a sleeping bag.

Rain asked him to help her.

She had been tired.

He dutifully obliged.

A Southern gentleman.

When it was all packed, the VW bug sputtering, she took a minute to place a guardian stone in front of her tipi and leave lots of food and water for the little cat that had shown up recently.

He caught a couple of mice, so Rain let him stay.

The cat watched the car drive off, sadly.

He could not help her from a distance.

His powers were not strong enough.

He would watch her things though.

He marveled at the small, lithe body he was in and enjoyed climbing a post, perching and looking out over the land.

He could see that the man with her was good though, so he relaxed and took a nap, waiting for her return.

"We need to stop down here at the pictographs."

"Oh, this has always drawn me, but I have never stopped."

"So, I am thinking that there is a cavern there. I thought this box was there, but I think it really is in **Medicine Rock.**"

"I have got to look here though, there are too many dreams and things, this necklace sings, and the objects show a dance. I have been practicing it, so we better stop. Maybe there is another clue."

"Sure thing, this is your trip, I am just here."

CHAPTER XXXI

I AM

"You can free yourself of your mind, which is the only
true liberation."

Eckhart Tolle
The Power of Now

She took another glance behind and around before making the final gestures in the dance to open the chambers.

Iam watched in fascination.

The objects had shown her how to do it, reflected in a Mirror, along with the singing necklace.

They showed the location and the dance.

Getting here had nearly cost her life and certainly had taken a large chunk of time.

What Rain had figured out from it all was that if she let any thoughts of dark in, the illusion remained.

She took a deep breath and imagined her roots extending into the ground, as a tree, and the tree drew in a breath of sunlight and exhaled it to the sky.

Her power began to grow and the wall began to dissolve below her carefully placed hands.

Each item in her amulet was glowing in turn with the moves.

The rock wall began to waver and dissolve as her turquoise eyes glittered with power, she again centered it and let go.

Stepping into the chamber, she knew she was in Her womb and had done the right thing.

The walls were adorned with the story of the times, her quest, the prophecies, and then Rain saw it.

It was her in many lifetimes, she knew now that her whole existence had been a predictable story.

The image upon the wall was as a mirror and in it she saw the Chroma reflecting.

It showed an image of a butterfly shaped rock, with a **vertical tunnel** into it and another exit, the Chroma was there.

Adorned with intricately carved Figures and symbols, the lid opened itself, revealing the doorway and key to Atlantis, but it was not in this cavern.

This was the mirror of the real location, at the opposite end.

Her people had hidden secrets in both places.

Ahomea, said to be the Mother of all Dragons, guarded both.

She was enormous and her power reached to either end.

They were connected.

Her people had run North when the threats had taken over.

One of the ancient pyramids had been buried below the mountain, and the doorway was here.

To protect the entry, two keys were needed.

The other key was a necklace that was often in her dreams.

It had animal fetishes and golden jaguar claws.

It was in the chest.

She heard the ancient rumble shiver down her soul.

She bowed in respect.

Here She was, the Mother Dragon.

She was kin, keeper of the family of Light, who were trained and ready to bring change.

They needed her to awaken though.

Too many hearts were blocked.

The fire of love She would breathe could clear this, instantly.

She also had suffered a sleeping potion of sorts, designed to last lifetimes.

This was the lifetime for awakening and removing the chips and blocks purposely placed upon the Dragon Riders of Atlantis and on their Mother Dragon.

This was the lifetime they were to win.

The cavern walls spoke the truth.

She needed to hurry.

The answer still was hidden in the chest.

The chest was not here, but her suspicion was right.

It was in Medicine Rock.

A sacred Blaze.

Sleepily Ahomea said,

"Child of Light, I am tired and they see me. You must hurry to my tail and activate the keys. We will all hold you and help, but you must do this alone. The one you are with will keep you safe for your trip. Combined energy is necessary, you must work in teams, but when you go to the chest, you go alone. Be swift."

She exited the wall that still seemed solid.

She had vanished into the rocks.

Iam breathed a sigh of relief.

He was not sure why, but he knew he had to protect this girl.

The story had made sense and called to him on a deep level.

He watched as she stumbled out, confused, with glittering eyes.

"We have to hurry."

They jumped in the VW, she gunned it down the bumpy road, as fast as she could.

She was in such a hurry, she did not see the black SUV fall in behind her.

"So, I need to tell you a bit about myself."

Rain fell into the story.

He listened quietly, letting her know he truly heard, by reflecting thoughtful questions.

"So, they told you, your test scores showed you was too smart, so they would not help."

"Yes, and my Mom, who is really wealthy, was helping, but one day, said she could not anymore. I was still looking for work, but had started getting panic attacks, and I had hurt myself long ago, at the hospital. I was kinda out of luck and about to be homeless. My depression was dark enough, I hardly cared."

"This fellow puts you on Backpage, and you were all right then"

"Well, yeah, a girl can earn lots of cash, if she looks nice and has a place."

He looked at her for a long minute.

"Well, seems like you are pretty smart."

Rain flushed.

The choices had not been many.

She had learned so much and was starting to accept why she studied this.

Rain saw challenges as lessons.

The sexual energy was one she needed to see all sides of.

Coming around from abuse and trauma to a feeling of control and power, then full circle to the compassion and understanding for the beautiful men who appeared on her table.

She taught them about their power, which helped shift the control game that the men needed to be taught to be Gods.

Women were coming back into power and ritual with Red Tent ceremonies and Goddess gatherings, but were neglecting to include the men.

Rain saw now, the problems had begun with a lack of balance with ceremony and ritual, and the labels and identifications with the sexes had caused a spilt.

The duality had begun.

"Iam, I need some money for traveling, my funds are about out."

She had been living frugally and off a small stash of cash.

It was about gone.

"I was not sure I wanted to, ever again, but I need to see clients."

"Sure, sugar, whatever ya'll need, I am here for you."

Rain sighed.

She could manage to see a bunch of clients, if she had help, and someone to hold space.

She would not advertise.

She had plenty of loyal customers who missed her style.

She could fill her wallet.

She borrowed his phone, sent a pile of texts and grinned as the usually quiet phone learned what it was like to be busy.

She even dared to text a couple who had pushed too hard and wanted more than she gave.

She felt strong enough, and Iam would be there.

The air was reasonably clean, the buzz of the city, intoxicatingly enchanting after the long quiet.

Snow still capped the Wasatch, the moon was almost full.

Pink was descending on the mountains as the sun dipped behind the lake.

Rain felt good being here.

She wanted to see Shelby Sky, tell her about the box, see the photographer who told her of the dream and to move through quickly.

The city looked and felt good, so a few days would be fine.

She needed the money.

She had the whole next day booked, which would cover the trip and her expenses for a month.

She could not worry about money, so this made sense, and the energy she raised was pleasant.

She had missed this side of herself.

The sexy, made-up Goddess, ready to make men scream in delight.

Being strong and masculine had been a great screen, but this side of her had power, though it still scared her.

She stared at herself in the mirror.

The mineral makeup made her eyes demand to be looked at.

They had been called eerie seeing deeply into souls.

A pink lacy push up bra did the trick under the low cut flowery dress.

Rain admired her nice cleavage, burying the giant quartz hanging on a necklace.

She turned and checked the lines of her dress and thigh-high, tattooed stockings, hidden below the hem, and thought to herself,

"Not too bad."

She had put on just enough weight and was tan from all the soaking, she was fresh and ready.

She felt the excitement build.

She fussed with the room, smudged and checked her makeup and sat, relaxed and ready.

She could hear the boots on the stairs but his knock was soft.

"Hey sugar, I missed you."

"You look amazing, I am so glad you texted me, I thought I was going to go insane here. I have lost all confidence in myself and am super stressed. Where on Earth have you been?"

"Here and there, now we can't have ya all balled up like this, hop on the table, and get cozy, be back in a sec."

He was on top of the silk sheet, which annoyed Rain, she liked to use the fabric to cover.

She would not touch her bare skin near buttocks or genitals, so she always draped them, once they were semi undressed and had climbed on top the table.

"Here honey, lift up"

She pulled it halfway on his legs.

Most of the guys relaxed more when covered, they knew it to be a signal for a happy end, though, so they stayed naked.

None of these guys had walked away unhappy, so she just smiled at the eagerness and slowed the pace.

Drawing it to the right moment was an art the young ones were not versed in.

She was lucky as she looked much younger than her age.

They got both youth and experience.

He moaned in pleasure as she slathered warm, scented coconut oil, and teased out the tension.

She worked on all parts, and began her sacred Lingam massage.

The penis had an energy system and an anatomy deep inside.

She liked reaching those places that are not usually touched.

She liked reminding them to run their energy and that the power they felt was their own.

She reminded them they were perfect, just as they were, made of love and light, and the energy raised was theirs alone, she was simply an antenna.

No fluid exchanged, just love and energy.

She did not allow herself to lose control to her needs.

It was not about her pleasure.

She tightly held her own reins, or the whole thing shifted.

By the end of the day, though, she could feel her own needs pulsing, and struggled not to give in to the desire with her last client.

He had previously asked her to date, but this time noticed his wedding ring. She smiled to herself.

She preferred married clients, as they were not interested in her outside of the hour.

He must have decided he did not want to date.

Good.

She imagined them going home relaxed, charged up, and ready to be present with their wives.

Those she knew would take it well, she reminded them to do something nice for her, treat her well.

Take the open heart and swept-out emotions home, be wonderful.

This was a service that kept many men happy, at home, disease free, yet satisfied in the human needs department.

She thought if she ever had a partner, and his needs were bigger than she wanted or needed to tend to, she would pay for it herself.

She would not be calling, expecting him to be there, play a game, give her more than some money and a tiny bit of his time and most of all, did not need to be lied to.

She could hardly believe the calm way Iam had just sat and waited.

He seemed impressed.

If he was turned on, he hid it well.

He was older and had worked in the marijuana industry long enough to appreciate the under-the-table and illegal business.

He took a glance at the cash she counted. One, two, three, four, five, six, seven hundred and forty dollars.

Not bad, for a skinny half-breed whom they told was too smart for her own good.

Well, perhaps they were right, she hid the already spoken for cash.

One more day, and they would have enough to head to Santa Fe.

Forrest was not expecting her this time.

She thought.

He fumed at his home.

He was not sure how to handle this.

He listened to the tapes again and again.

She had found it.

She was seeing clients.

He was not ready to part with it.

The secrets too deep.

He was so tired lately, this girl was ruining it for him.

He had underestimated her.

Now she knew his secret resting place from the public and the law.

A couple objects were under investigation.

As long as they were hidden, Forrest was safe, so were the powerful objects.

He had studied her profile carefully and ordered the surveillance early in her search.

Since she worked as a sensual healer, he knew she could keep secrets. She was smart, had an RN license, several black belts, spoke German fluently, and a tenacious will to live.

He admired her grit.

This was an apparently dangerous girl, this Reagan Bauer.

He saw her as just that, but had not anticipated this.

He would move the chest.

She had written, asking about camping there.

Why had he told her she could?

He had wanted her where he knew she would be.

He had lost his mind.

He replied to her.

"Rain, I am selling the ruins. Somebody has already made payments, and is building out there."

She had seen a building when they were there before.

It was at about mile eight.

He was hiding from her.

He had already told her she could camp there.

They would swim in the creek, he had said.

"I do not feel well, my Doctor told me I cannot be on my computer so much."

"OK, Forrest."

Rain plotted.

Whether she would tell or not, he had not decided.

She seemed unpredictable.

The council assured him, she was to be the One.

He had been guarding this secret for too long.

He did not know what to do with her.

For the first time in years, a wave of anxiety washed over Forrest Fenn.

Rain knew what she would have to do.

Go get it.

Down nine miles of harsh desert road.

On private property.

It definitely was too far to walk.

Rain heard it again.

"Some secrets are best left alone."

This was the final clue Rain had needed to know.

She knew the Chroma was in there, despite the threats, despite the quest saying North of Santa Fe.

It was secret.

A place Forrest loved.

Riches old and new lay quietly waiting to tell or not.

He watched the sun setting, often, from Medicine Rock.

Certainly, a marvel gaze.

She was finished seeing clients, she had enough to get by for a minute. Since she had only seen established clients, she was under the radar.

Andy had been out of town, his email said, but then he would know she traveled with a man.

He would be furious.

He was illogically jealous.

Rain was leery when his email said, "I hope your trip was productive."

He knew she needed money and had sounded disappointed when she said she felt better.

Being in the city was getting to her.

Shelby was going to meet them, then the plan was to leave.

Rain's head hurt and her lower left lung had air leaking out, again.

Salt Lake just was not healthy for her, but the energy had been fun, and the stimulation appreciated.

Wondering who was out to get her made her sicker.

She imagined most of it, she breathed.

They would be gone in an hour, or so.

Shelby operated on Indian time, predictably 45 minutes late, but perfectly calm.

She was a breath of fresh air, breezing in with a pretty silk, multi-layered, wrap around, knee-high skirt, bangles and a yellow scarf.

"So sorry, I am late, oh so good to see you."

She squeezed Rain.

Shelby was one of the few women she felt really close to and able to be physical with.

Rain melted in the warm, vanilla scent, hugging her friend back tightly.

"I missed you so much!"

"This is Iam."

The two hugged and Rain could see the instant connection.

Excited.

Rain filled Shelby in on all of the details.

Shelby was just as enamored with Forrest as Rain was, and giggled at the story.

"You lucky girl."

"I know, right, " Rain flushed.

Then remembered,

"But he is lying about the chest, and the resting place, something is wrong, and he is ignoring me. He said he was sick, but posted a blog about going to Suzanne Somer's Palm Spring home. He met Barry Manilow and some other fancy people. Barry wants to look for the chest. Man, we are in a hurry here and dealing with Forrest shutting me out."

"I can leave whenever."

Shelby brightened, thinking.

"We may be trespassing to go get it, but I think he might admire that, as long as we never say anything." Rain said.

"This will be a full-on Rambo mission."

"What?"

"Dark clothes, radios, hiding. We will need to plan it really well."

"Oh," she giggled, "Fun, we are going on an adventure."

"Yes, Ma'am."

Both Rain and Iam said together.

"Just so you know, let me show you how the poem works to get right to the exact spot. Just like he said, someone would go right to it. He just, like, did not think it would be yet. The whole first stanza is clue Numero Uno.

"He goes there three times a week, by himself. There are treasures old and new. This tells you it is on his land.

"So, we figured out the poem is directions.

"In his new book, the map goes from Canada right down to where his ruins are. People used to travel these ways all the time. The Santa Fe Trail was a trading route. Only a few landmarks were needed.

"It is below the home of Brown, or literally, the San Juan Pueblo.

"Heavy loads and water high, a giant rock with a ship perched on top, Shiprock. Take the left trail, nigh, then look for the blaze.

"Medicine Rock was how the people found this camp. It was a magical blaze for ceremonies. Stand on it, there is a tunnel, look quickly down, don't stand on top gazing, dodo, and go in the tunnel. Be brave, it is cold, and there are snakes and spiders. On the altar shelf, get past the woody pack rat's nest, and there is the chest."

Her words ran together.

Shelby was bouncing in her chair.

"He gets energy off of this search, and people admiring him, his work. As long as people look for it, it feeds him. Can you keep this secret for Forrest?"

"I would love to have his permission to go and look, but he is being weird."

"The thing is, too, I do not know why, but he has been different. He was all about me coming, camping on the land, and hanging out with him. As soon as he knew I was traveling with someone, his energy shifted."

"He somehow knows just what I am doing."

"I am not sure what he would do, if we trespassed and got caught.

He might enjoy the publicity, but then again he could just press charges. He is bound to have it monitored. He said he would know for sure, but on the land itself, he may not think anyone would walk in."

"I have an advantage, since I have been there, but I was being polite about the gate codes, and looked away, I could have seen in the reflection of the window, but we will not be driving anyway, so oh well. I should have watched though."

"I mean, ya'll, I could be wrong, I have been looking and coming up empty, when I thought I had it. It could be another dead end, or a trap. The cavern in Montana, plainly shows Medicine Rock and the magic within the chest. I almost fear opening the thing, with all the talk about voodoo curses and what it showed."

"A huge shift happens when it gets opened, it unlocks the keys to the mystery of the power of the human heart. The energy of this power is why we have been repressed. We are infinitely powerful and magical. The Serpent influence, Sagiditis, will be forever banished and harmony is restored."

Shelby shifted in her chair, but kept her green eyes fastened on Rain.

"Oh yeah, we win, we win!"

"This is why we are all here during this time, to save the planet. As ambassadors of the Family of Light, we are here to take back our planet, once and for all. We have all been in training for lifetimes. This is it. Are we ready?"

The pep talk worked.

Everyone was talking at once, excitedly.

"So, we will have to plan this really well, and need a team to do it. "

"When do we leave?"

They sat around the small, wooden kitchen table and discussed the plans until early in the morning.

The man listened intently, and thought he might just race ahead of them. The chest had more value than the rich man was paying him. He just quit, he thought. He sent a quick text to his employer.

"Nothing new..."

Forrest received the text.

He knew the man was lying, and decided what to do with him. He would catch him closer to home.

He understood deception, but would not be cheated.

Forrest twisted his hands.

He tried the breathing techniques so useful when panicking.

"Peggy, will you bring me a glass of ice water please?"

"Of course, sweetheart, what is wrong?"

She was worried, he looked pale, and had been getting more tired lately. The doctor had told her, privately, he was worried. The lab tests were mysterious.

The doc was worried, but knew Forrest would stress, so told Peggy to watch him closely, and report back.

"What can I do for you?"

"Nothing."

He snapped.

He saw her react and realized his mistake.

"Oh honey, I am sorry. Let's go fishing."

She packed a lunch and her book she was reading and hopped in the jeep. They headed towards Chama, Forrest quiet, but calm.

He needed to think, fishing helped him do this.

Peggy was glad he seemed calmer, but still worried. She rested her hand on his and closed her eyes and prayed.

She was his rock, and he never would have lived without her love and support.

This he knew.

She understood him.

Knew him.

Loved him with such depth, it still surprised her.

He was always calm and loving after fishing.

Until Rain.

This one was bothering him.

He had felt so badly for her after the research he had done.

It would be hard not to, given the surveillance he had tapped into.

His curiosity and his own paranoia had led him to contact old friends of his.

He knew everything about her, before he agreed to meet her.

She had a public blog, and wrote nice things about him.

She never revealed their secrets, blogging innocently and not even asking for a picture.

A few people had seen them together, but mostly she was as secretive as he was.

To her credit, she was good at throwing others off her trail, and kept it light and fun.

He thought maybe she would just take it and go in peace.

He was considering his options when his phone chimed he had an email.

"Forrest, are you OK? Your energy is different, do you still want me to come? I am sulking. --r"

"Don't sulk, Rain, I have an appointment. --ff"

She was getting pushy, it annoyed him.

He thought that would hold her for a minute.

He enjoyed making her wait and seeing how she responded.

He laughed, later when he heard her fuming about Suzanne Somers and the party he had been to.

"An appointment? With Palm Springs. Yeah, not feeling well, are we Forrest..."

Keeping up with her was tiring him more, his excuses were running out.

He tossed his line in and let it drift downstream.

He was pleased when he hooked a huge fish and let it go.

Knowing he held the life in his hands felt powerful and it refreshed his energy.

He felt good for the first time in a few weeks.

For a few minutes he forgot about Reagan Bauer.

When he got home, he answered another email.

"Amy, when are you coming to New Mexico, I will give you my book."

This searcher had been contacting him.

Amy was writing a blog that Forrest liked.

He read it again, and replied in the chat room under his searching pen name.

He kept up with the chatter by pretending to be a searcher.

He found out all sorts of things people thought about him like that.

"He never put it out there, he is just feeding a sick ego."

To which he replied,

"Don't spoil the fun, of course it is out there, the point is looking, it is just too hard for ya...lol."

"Forrest Fenn is just after publicity and money from the book."

"Hey numb nut, he donates all the profits and the publicity has died down."

"Yeah, what about the voodoo curse on it?"

"Rubbish."

"Rubbish?"

"Who are you?"

The blog chat room exploded with angry chatter.

Forrest left the room, pleased.

He emailed Amy and asked her if she had found anything.

She was off to West Yellowstone to look below Hebgen Dam, where nine of Osborne Russell's men fell, and find that box.

Amy had only been looking for seven months but was excited, and thought she would be the wise one to figure it out.

She ran her short fingers through a spiky blonde pixie cut, working the tension out.

She scrolled through the blogs and comments, looking for new threads, but saw none.

Closing her silver-stickered iMac, and packing the rest of her tattered backpack with less than she wanted, Amy was ready.

She made sure her flashlight and pepper spray were on top, loaded her black Toyota Four Runner, and headed down the greening Gallatin Canyon towards Hebgen Lake.

She stopped at the Cinnamon Lodge and had a medium-rare bison burger for lunch, enjoyed the banter with the owner, Ryan, and asked if he would discount any of his photography.

"I can come down some."

She wanted the grizzly shot for her downtown office in Bozeman. She was a new lawyer and was decorating still, but struggling with finances after school, establishing herself.

"That one is nice. I will have to come back later, when I have found my treasure."

"Oh, treasure?"

Amy told him about "the Thrill."

"Oh, come to think of it, last Summer, an old ski patrol friend stopped in, She was looking for that box too. Hum, maybe I will have to look it up. What did you say the guy's name was again?"

"Forrest Fenn."

"Oh yeah, gotcha. OK cool. I will scope it out when I get a minute. "

Amy wondered when that would be, seeing the frantic way he was having to keep up with the food and alcohol orders. Then again, less competition was OK. She was becoming irritated by other searchers looking for her box. Knowing anyone could look was one thing. She was getting attached to the idea of being the wisest one of them all.

She hooked a left, and continued towards Hebgen.

A yellow jeep with New Mexico plates passed her. She could hear the reggae blaring.

The guy looked off.

Amy backed up and gave him room.

She sped up when she had thought about the plates and maybe this guy was looking too.

"Slow down, enjoy the views."

She turned off the radio. NPR was getting scratchy. Her CD player had broken last month. It would be the first thing she bought with her money. Amy liked listening to something to keep her head from being too busy. She rolled the window down instead, and let the still chilled air flood in.

She was careful not to speed once in the park, and laughed as she saw the curly headed man from New Mexico arguing with the Park Rangers outside his jeep.

This was not going to be good for him, she chuckled.

Better to be patient and enjoy the view.

A friend had shown her *The Thrill of the Chase*, hoping it would distract her from her depression and anxiety.

Finishing school had been a challenge after some serious life events had gotten her down.

Chasing the box had given her the spark needed to finish the last few months of graduating and hard studying for the Bar Exam.

She had passed on the first go, and was allowing a trip before she got serious.

No way was anything going to distract her.

She had read about nine of Osborne Russell's men falling there.

There was another blogger who left very helpful tidbits.

Amy followed the blog closely, and thought the one who wrote *Up a Cold Creek Without a Paddle*, might just be the one who was within five hundred feet of the box and did not know it.

There were good pictures of a blaze and the woman had laughingly said, "Go for it."

Amy knew she would search more carefully and not miss it.

"Forrest, I have not found it, but I will bring you your bracelet, when I can come there. I have to find the box."

"Where are you looking?"

She told him, hoping for a reaction.

She could not see his shoulders shrug in resignation, but perked up at,

"Amy, good luck, keep your eyes on the ground."

"Darn it," he thought.

He looked for Rain's GPS signal from her car and within her body. They were moving in opposite directions.

The car was in St. Louis.

What was she doing?

He honed in on her tracker.

It said Salt Lake City.

"What on Earth?"

He listened carefully.

Rain was on her way already.

The plans had been carefully gone over, again and again.

The four of them would be going into the ruins in three nights.

They were taking separate vehicles.

Rain was not in her car.

Shelby was driving it.

Iam drove Shelby's old cop car, she had bought it at an auction, then painted it wildly.

It was not a discrete car, but it never had been online, so was a mystery.

It would take awhile to figure out who was driving and who it belonged to.

The ancient cruiser was registered under Shelby's Mom, who used several names.

She had been doing so since the Sixties.

Blue Bell, it was now, had a talent.

She could locate foreign objects in humans and remove them.

Rain had been scanned and cleaned.

A fat, scruffy, tabby who had been unfortunate enough to be wandering by, now sported a fancy, microscopic tracker that he greedily scarfed down with tuna.

His nightly rounds showed him by Whole Foods, Omar's Rawtopia, and Barnes and Noble.

Kind of late for Rain, but not that noticeable, for a minute.

The time game had begun.

The fourth member of the team was a friend of Shelby's.

He was quiet, with an intent gaze.

Adam had sandy blonde wavy hair down to his shoulders.

He wore it pulled back with a dark brown leather tie.

His blue-green eyes stared intently, listening deeply.

Shelby thought he was perfect.

"He is a ninja, I have known him all my life. He is as dedicated to saving Gaia as we are."

"All right, bring him in. We need to get him up to speed."

Adam strode in, an hour later, still lanky with adolescence, wiry strength was evident in his long limbs.

Rain took him in, gazed into his eyes and felt the power and kindness in the youth, and figured he would do just right.

"Shelby said we are going to have a bit of fun, no?"

He had a slight accent.

Rain wondered where he was from.

It was hard to tell.

She usually could pin an accent, she spoke a few languages and could imitate pretty well.

"Yeah, you ready?"

"She told you to pack light, right?"

He just had a small green backpack, hardly big enough for a day pack.

"I don't ever need much."

Rain loved traveling with experienced road warriors.

This was going to be fun, dangerous, but fun.

Rain wondered what Forrest would actually do if he caught them on the ruins.

She knew she had an advantage, but the rest of her team did not.

He may be even angrier with her, if she broke his trust.

Worrying was not helping.

Nervous tension bit into her shoulders, they scrunched tightly, her jaw worked knots into her cheek.

They needed to hurry, Rain spotted a black SUV getting closer and closer. She could feel a strangely confused energy coming from the rig.

She knew that if she had thought of this answer, she was not alone. That was the way the thoughtmosphere worked.

The potential lines of communication between human hearts ran in energetic lines, much as a web, around the Universe.

The crew agreed to meet at Pagosa Springs for the final leg.

They would leave Shelby's car there, and go in one.

The gear was piled, and they rode in quiet wonder.

It was so pretty in this part of the country.

The red stones drifted into the softer pastels of the southern desert.

Georgia O'Keeffe painted them famously.

They passed the historical marker reminding them of her greatness.

Past Chama, past the turnoff for Ojo Caliente, they edged into Santa Fe.

Turning up the road to the ski hill, the air turned cooler.

They quickly set up camp at the campground.

Tall pines blanketed the sky, as the sun began to dip behind the horizon.

The team was hopeful.

Edgy.

Nerves thick, but laughter echoed anyway.

"I just love the desert. I really did not know how many mountains there were here, though. Super cool," Adam said, doing a funny dance.

Everyone chuckled.

It was pretty empty, except for a large, older, broken RV down at the end.

The weather was too cold for most tourists, still.

Everyone was a bit shaken up, laughter a relief.

Just as they had been approaching town, there had been a nasty wreck.

A black SUV had been following closely.

Around a sharp bend, Rain had looked back in time to see the front left tire explode.

The huge car had tumbled off the road.

She had seen another car stop, so she kept going.

It had looked like a small bomb had hit the car.

Rain had been seeing it for too long and had been watching it.

She had grown used to seeing it.

She hoped the driver was OK.

He moaned inside the rig, alive.

He would not be going after the chest.

Forrest laughed from his perch.

He had not fired that gun in ages.

It made such a nice mess.

That ought to keep him away.

He knew the SUV he paid for would keep the man safe, so he was not worried.

He was tired and needed to go home.

Peggy would be wondering what was taking him so long getting a grouse.

He would arrive empty-handed and she would have to cook him something else.

What a great life.

He just wished he were not getting so tired and dizzy.

It scared him.

He still had not decided what do about the thieving crew.

He was trying to pin their location, since Rain had ditched the trackers.

It did not take him long to figure it out.

He had other ways of finding her.

Shelby had not turned off her phone.

Forrest had gotten the number long ago when she joined the hunt.

Shelby was coming south.

Forrest figured Rain was not far.

She was the leader.

He did tell people they could have it.

Nobody should have figured it out.

Maybe, the Council was correct.

He would wait and see.

If he had them arrested out there, it would go public, regardless.

This could be good.

Or devastating.

His friend in the Government assured him Rain was still not in trouble.

They had watched her, knew about her, but thought she was quiet enough, respectful and the officers had great performance days after seeing her for a massage.

She was being considered for a position in some very secret places.

They continued to monitor for just a while.

They needed her better and just waited to see how she would make it.

He had not counted on her ancient abilities.

This could not be researched where Forrest could find it.

Forrest and his search were a hot show aboard the ship, but he did not have access to the same information.

They had tried to lure him in with all sorts of enticing art.

He had not bitten, as he was well-protected and informed.

He owed nothing, got nothing.

The stone, they had tried to steal back, but had never been able to get in.

The magical items in his home, protected his property well.

Since he had held the ancient portal key, he carried a unique charge that repelled the serpents.

He was well-protected on energetic levels.

Physically, he faded, though he felt this with a sickening dread.

The one thing he feared most was death.

He had cheated it several times and thought he should again.

Forrest twisted his hands.

The right person to hold the secrets, his mission.

They weighed him down.

Tiring.

"I have done it tired, now I am weak."

Turning up the road to the ski hill, Rain remembered her first meeting with Forrest.

He had driven her up here.

They had parked at one of the recreational parking spots and talked.

She had loved his gentle ways.

"Rain, I think you need to relax."

Rain stared at him intensely.

"I will relax when I find the box."

Forrest sighed.

At least she was determined.

What if they got it out first?

What if this was the wrong team?

Time would mirror the reflection of answer.

With the precautionary traps he had set, they would be lucky to get it out at all.

Tera, his favorite rattler, stood ultimate guard.

He felt kinda bad for the cute girl, but still wondered what punishment he would be giving for her deception, but still hoping she made it.

The quest was always a double-edged blade.

He ran through the various scenarios in his mind, hoping she really was the right one.

She was going to go get it.

He watched the BLM maps flash, and saw the access, Wagon Wheel Road, come up and get locked into.

He saw them looking at Cache Creek Ranch Road.

Moving the maps around on both sides.

The combined private and BLM land.

Both points were gated.

He laughed.

"Good luck," he snickered.

Way too far to walk.

Adam had been posted outside Forrest's home now, since before he was able to get home.

They had dropped him earlier, with the bike.

He saw Forrest pull in and unload a big gun.

He made a call, his wife brought him an iced tea.

"Charmay, do you have the monitors on out at the ruins?"

"Forrest, hon, they always are, nothing will bother your stuff, what is wrong with you, sugar?"

"Nothing."

She hung up, puzzled, in her small, modern yellow kitchen.

Adam had snuck as close as he could and had a good view of the monitor.

"Oh, crap."

He watched the footage of them coming south streamed onto the screen.

He saw himself hop on the bike.

It dawned on him he better get out of there.

He hurried back and pedaled furiously.

"The man knows everything."

"It does not change our plans."

"We rise before 5 a.m. this morning and begin."

The time came before anyone was ready.

Their watches lined up.

2:55 a.m.

Matching the landscape, each of them set about their tasks.

By 3:17 a.m., they were out the door.

Radios working.

"One check."

"Copy one."

"Two check."

"Copy two."

They left the car and set out on foot to the rental they stashed.

Nerves ran thick.

Tension dripped them with sweat.

The tapes began playing back in the tent.

It gave them almost three hours.

It took forty to drive behind the ruins.

The walk in was long, they needed horses.

They stuck by the creek bed.

Careful, on the BLM land, to stay low.

This land was carefully watched.

They snuck in behind a car entering.

Saw the puzzled look in the rearview mirror, and the shrug.

The car was nice enough.

Rain slowed enough to not look alarming.

The maroon Isuzu kept going.

The plan was working.

The horses had been left, tied.

Iam's connection was happy to help the pirating crew.

He wanted the gold dragon.

He could have it.

The information had been hidden, protected from the public eyes.

Though public land, the address carefully restricted.

All access extremely difficult.

Rain had an advantage, though.

CHAPTER XXXII

THE WAY IN

"The foot feels the foot when it feels the ground."

Buddha

She had been there. She never forgot features in the landscape.

Though Rain had been polite about the gate codes, she had been memorizing the land.

Deep down, she knew she would be back.

She had walked here centuries before.

Had fought for her people's right to perform Magic.

They had run, after the revolt in **1680**.

The guilt at the rage.

The karma of the Wheel irreparably ripped.

The once peaceful People had killed.

A sickness had descended on their hearts.

It was time to undo the damage. Repair the rip.

Adam was posted by the front road.

Near the horse rescue ranch.

He was "working."

Shelby tucked herself behind a large rock outcrop near where they parked in Wagon Wheel.

She was high on a bluff and could see three hundred and sixty degrees.

Once the signal to disperse was sent, each was to go different directions.

Shelby left her phone at the campground.

It would stay there.

With the rest of the gear.

They would meet back at Pagosa in one day.

Rain and Iam walked quietly towards Medicine Rock on the two small horses.

Studying maps, they had decided on this way.

The horses they rented from a private rancher who Iam had connections with, would be the only way.

The rancher was happy to help.

Treasure and a deep suspicion regarding Forrest was enough.

Coming in from behind the rock minimized the trespassing.

It would just be Forrest and a couple families who might care.

"I think we are about there."

She could barely see the hand movements.

They had come up with a few to communicate.

Talking would be a bad idea.

She thought he might have game cameras or voice-activated monitors.

He had both.

She signaled him to come closer.

She pointed to a low-lying camera attached to a post.

They walked the horses around a rock to get behind it.

Back at camp, the tape played.

They were just getting up and discussing getting to the Ruins.

There it was, shining, even in the dimly lit night.

Medicine Rock.

Her heart picked up the pace and she felt fear.

Sweat began to bead.

There were snakes and spiders in that dark, cold tunnel.

"What a dumb idea, I do not think I am wise." Rain doubted.

Fear sunk to her toes.

Dripping sweat.

Her breath came quicker.

Felt hard to get.

"Calm down. This is it." She soothed herself.

Rumors of murders and treasures long ago.

Fictional, but rumored.

"A hint of riches old and new."

Rain had to go in.

She thought maybe this was a bad idea, and thought about turning around.

"Shit, shit, shit, this is it, now or never, it is in there or not, you die or not, just do it, you chicken."

The internal dialog started.

Her heart hammered.

The stone felt cold, full of warning.

She flashed on a different time.

She had touched this before.

Helped build it.

The secrets were here.

"Keep going."

One arm.

The next.

In she crawled.

Squinting her eyes shut for a second.

Rain swallowed her fear.

She stopped.

Paralyzed.

She wanted out.

Horrified at where she was that moment.

Allowing the puckering in her body to dissipate, with deep breathing.

Each inch taking her closer to her destiny.

She moved forward.

"You will learn a big life lesson if you go in there," Forrest had warned.

Slowly.

The headlamp sickly dim.

There was not enough light.

Not enough air.

Breathing deeply, she calmed herself.

She had to stay focused.

Grounded.

She inched forward.

Spiderwebs in front of her.

Dust and dirt fell with each slide.

She sneezed.

Something moved.

The radio crackled.

Three keys on the mic.

Someone one was coming.

Rain did not care.

Deeply in.

Too deep.

"Be brave," she whispered to the walls.

She slid forward.

She would not stop now.

Her amulet was floating above her neck.

The music she had not heard since Atlantis.

A glow began.

Rain noticed a small, thin string across the tunnel.

She crept below it.

She was small and able to contort.

Iam watched her from his belay spot.

She reached the chamber.

Rain did not take long to look around.

She knew there were at least a few snakes, it was cold.

They should be slow.

As she approached the altar ledge, the music hummed.

The sound of a rattle was suddenly louder.

She sat coiled, just in front of the ledge.

Rain approached slowly.

The snake got louder.

She tossed a stone, the snake flew at it.

This gave Rain the chance she needed.

Rain pinned it down with a long stick she had dragged in and cut the head off with her giant knife.

Finally the weight of it on her leg made sense.

She did not care for killing, and said a prayer for the snake.

In her dreams, this one had bitten her.

The sacred shelf.

It was covered in a thickly-wooded pack rat nest.

Magic covered in grime.

Rain cringed.

Her thick leather gloves felt thinner than they were.

She reached into the thick nest towards the back.

Spiny cactus jammed into her gloves.

Below this was an arrangement of crystals, shells, arrowheads, a turtle, a pipe, and an odd stone.

That was it?

It could not be empty.

Rain reached back farther.

An edge.

Metal.

She could feel the cold through the gloves.

The excitement coursed through her.

She was going home.

Pulling it out.

The nest fell to the ground.

"Oh my Goddess, it is freaking here. It is here. The Chroma."

Her heart soared.

She felt the tears well.

"Oh, it is so beautiful."

The bronze was dirty, but the figures adorning it seemed to dance, waving.

Rain was mesmerized.

A quick exhale as she tried to contain her giddiness.

She was at the bottom of a vertical shaft, on private property, stealing a treasure chest worth untold millions of dollars.

She heard Forrest saying, "Rain, it is North of Santa Fe."

She giggled with tension and disbelief.

Glad she had listened to her instinct.

Getting out was next.

Four keys.

Four times.

They found it.

Quickly, Rain moved the rest of the mess of the nest.

Placed it back together as best she could, on the ground.

Rain dusted the altar items, gave thoughts and prayers, thanks.

She was paying ancient homage to the power bundle and by cleaning it, activating the power within.

Energy raced through her.

The song loudly echoing in the cavern.

She started to sway and hum.

Pulled towards opening the lid, hypnotized.

She shook herself.

They were not going to open it yet.

The heavy, bronze chest was dirty.

The bits of wood fell on the ground.

Beady eyes glared at her.

She could not help but shiver.

She put it into the dark purple magically protective satchel, hooked it to the rope and tugged.

Out it lifted on the pulley.

Iam struggled with the weight, lifting it upwards inch-by-inch.

Charmay was pulling in right then.

She was confused about Forrest's behavior, and wanted to check the game cameras.

She came here to think too.

She thought she had seen something on the way in, but she figured it was her imagination or one of the many ghosts.

Nobody would dare be here, alone, especially at night.

She scanned the lightening hillsides and sighed.

She missed her friend.

He had been so distant.

They used to have so much fun together here.

She thought the lock box key he gave her to look into, only upon his death held the answers.

Maybe she would break her promise.

She had a suspicion it held deeply hidden answers.

He had told her he was steering the public away from his resting place.

She knew where he wanted his bones.

She was to look in the lock box only after his death.

He had made her swear.

He was selling this place, did not feel good, and was ignoring her.

He had been so paranoid.

She wanted to know what he was hiding.

No way would she walk up there in the dark, so she sipped coffee from her green metal thermos, watched the sun come up and waited.

Rain and Iam quickly rode back to the well-hidden rental car, left the horses tied where he said they would, hopped in and drove North.

His connection would get the horses by daybreak.

The chest was buried in the protective bag, deep in the underbelly, where the spare was.

It begged to be looked at.

Too bright back there.

A few miles away from the ruins, Rain said.

"Nobody is following us."

"Stop. We have to give Forrest his bracelet."

"Pull over behind the mall."

"Rain, that is not a good idea, we need to get out of here."

"You are right, but we still need to give him his bracelet."

"Yes Ma'am, I agree, but ya'll don't wanna get stuck now."

"Oh crap, you are right again. Keep going."

She watched for cars that followed.

They drove north, as planned, after meeting at the edge of town.

Changing the plans that were placed verbally.

The true plan had been written only.

Never spoken.

Burned once read.

The load in the trunk begging to be opened and admired.

It was tortuous leaving it back there.

Several times on the ride, one team member or the other wanted to look right then.

"Just freakin' pull over for a second, Rain, I have to pee and we should look."

"Remember, we need to make a circle, to open it, safety first, ya'll, let's burn one," Iam said.

Forrest woke, confident the "team" was just rising for coffee, as this was what the audio tape played.

They were laughing about the chest, the quest and never finding it.

He had easily found them with Shelby's phone.

Shelby used it often to text and Facebook, making it easier to track. He had a sinking feeling he could not explain.

Just to be sure, he went to his secret monitoring room.

The weighted sensor was empty.

He had slept through it.

He played the video feeds.

They had been well-hidden, quiet.

Eluded him by riding horses.

Playing the tape.

He saw her kill his snake.

He saw her hook the chest, in the odd and old looking bag.

He saw it rise.

He saw them leave with it.

Then she was in his face.

Smiling.

"Hi, Forrest," she mouthed.

"Hugs!"

He had been beaten.

He opened the blogs.

Hers was quiet, and put her in West Yellowstone, looking by Hebgen Lake under a different blaze.

Where her first item had been.

They had his treasure.

All of the tracking devices were saying different things or were still and silent.

He knew she was on the run.

He was furious.

She had fooled him.

He hoped they were careful.

He hoped this crew was going to do the right thing.

He needed to feel better, he swallowed an aspirin and bellowed for Peggy to bring him the paper.

She was getting frustrated with his attitude and told him it was still by the drive.

He should get it himself.

This was going to be a long day.

He was too tired to get up.

Driving carefully, they passed the famously painted landscapes, hardly noticing.

The Chroma rested in the trunk.

Quietly humming within the satchel containing it, waiting to tell the secrets.

Her amulet was actively humming a soft and low hum.

"Ahomea."

It stretched into these sounds.

The colors were bright, birds sang loudly.

As they passed, the trees bowed their branches in waves of ecstatic dancing.

Gaia could be set free.

The sky and ground kissed, the Sun and Moon remembered the People.

A waking yawn descended as She opened her eyes and Saw.

Her Children cared.

Navapachute was a good place to open the Chroma.

The root Chakra of Ahomea was here.

Tribes had shared this place of power and healing for centuries.

The awakened Rainbow Flower Soldiers would gather to begin returning the Power items.

It had begun after they had moved from the great islands in the South Pacific.

Before the three tribes that recently had shared the place of Power, they had been there.

The Sacred Places had been recreated.

Temples built.

Doorways left.

It would begin again.

According to the Wheel of Law, all Temples were schools first, then for Spirituality.

The first Sun Dance in their new home had been here.

The four warriors had agreed then, to do this now.

The portal they needed had been created on a different spin on time's circle.

Keys left.

This would be the first doorway opened, allowing information to stream into human consciousness.

Sacred information waited to be allowed in.

The channel could be changed to the right frequency, the Wheels spinning correctly.

The newly visible energy circles forming around their feet would carry each of the four in the directions needed.

The Medicine Wheel was awakened.

Estcheemah and Blue Hair knew who they were.

Tomahseeasah was ready for the Power her challenges had brought her.

Lighting Bolt knew he had done the right thing.

The Serpent Mother had taught them all well.

"Estcheemah taught me that human ignorance and fear are our greatest enemies. Humans will do anything, including murder, to escape self-responsibility. This is why so many in our world are confused about who they are. She had the courage to speak of Creation, "Life is precious." Maturity must be gained before we can do any kind

of justice to matters of greatness. In this culture, we are taught to reduce the profound to the tangible. Expand the teachings into the vastness and ancient Self Discipline she taught."

The attempt to ignore our Creator Mother Goddess is the most crippling blow that all of humanity has ever suffered. The true and absolute Balance of our Creator Mother and Father is the most Holy and Powerful symbol and reality that can be known to humanity."

Paraphrased from Hymyeosos Storm by Lighting Bolt

Iam pulled out a booklet.

"I am alive."

He read to them, while they drove the rest of the three hours.

Lighting Bolt had written Iam's tribe, the KeeOkee.

"A true teacher never binds you with his will, he always works to set you free."

The booklet said,

Dear Brothers and Sisters,

My Friends, when one song becomes clear, you must look to our Mother Earth for Another Singer. She loves you and everywhere are her beautiful signs for you to learn. You need no Medicine Person, bible, book, established religion or social law or teachings to show you yourself. The mirrors of perception are everywhere for you. There are the tangled things of this world, pain and foolishness, but it is in this way that you learn your Personal Powers. These Powers are promised to you by your Heart. Sweet Medicine if you will walk your Own Path and listen to the song of the Universe. It is the way you will See the Lodge of Fulfillment our Mother Earth provided for you.

Go to no man. Follow no person. Question everything. Walk your own path. Learn to Sing your own songs. Question every god placed before you. Gods are social images that can twist your Path to the point where you will not know yourself where it is you Walk.

Become a Shaman, I tell you this, I truly mean it. Heal yourselves and then you can heal others. Protect your Dreams and learn to love yourself. If you do not care for yourself, then how can you care for anything or anyone else? Be at peace with yourself, my Friends, and seek the SEVEN ARROWS of your own Medicine. Be Wise enough to perceive beyond your own tiny circle of Firelight. Listen to your Heart and Talk with your Psyche, both are your guides.

You have a Vision Quest, it is within you. Life can be an adventure of discovery and living or it can be an endless job of trying to fit or trying to "make it," it is your choice which path you follow. If we should ever meet, let it be as equals and Brothers. Peace to you and those you love. Rainbow Around you as your Comforter. Say your own words and the People will see you Sun Dance.

Peace,

Hyemeyohysts

The crew arrived in Pagosa.

Frazzled, wired, paranoid and overly excited to open the box.

Nerves ran thick.

Tempers were quick.

"Freakin' A! Are we ever going to get there?" Shelby complained.

"We are here. Not much longer, OK, breathe," Rain answered.

"This is so intense," Adam said in his strange accent.

The car erupted in laughter.

Adam was good to slice tension with jokes.

Rain could see his jaw tightening, though, as he scanned for cars following.

As planned, they divided, then met again at the hotel.

They were at the Healing Waters Spa, in Room 16.

Having circled around all of the buildings several times.

Each approached.

Shelby was to check the room, Rain waited with the chest.

Trying to appear nonchalant was challenging, when a group of giddy girls ran by to go jump in the pools.

Hardly able to contain the thrill at opening the box.

"Rain, for crap sake, I cannot wait any longer."

Shelby breathed down Rain's neck.

"Go in and look, Shelby. Close the blinds, give the signal if we are good," Rain instructed.

The crew had been careful to watch for cars following them.

Nobody had seen any.

Shelby scouted the room and blinked the lights three times.

It was safe to take the beautiful bronze box inside.

It was really heavy.

"Gosh, this thing weighs a ton."

Rain hurried inside with it.

They pulled the curtains and latched all three locks.

The group huddled closely.

They smudged and grounded, already feeling the shift in energy.

Sagiditis was gone.

The prophecies fulfilled.

Without seeing or knowing the battle behind, it had been done.

If the chest opened, and they were near, the whole ship would evaporate.

Sagiditis knew about this too late.

Carefully constructed mirrored lies had been in place since the arrival and knowledge of this.

Shankar had high-tailed it back to the void, searching another planet to target, just before the Ahomea awoke.

A stream of curses followed in the wake of the ship.

The final straw had been drawn.

Universal Council could banish the Sagiditis, forever to the void.

It was done.

The Chroma was cold.

Decorated beautifully.

Women dancing.

Old world magic.

The latch stuck.

"Oh, no. It will not move, hold on," she said.

Rain used a knife to loosen it, carefully.

Dabbed olive oil into the hole with a Q-Tip.

It popped.

All four gaped as the lid opened.

Silence descended and stayed.

Many minutes of excited disbelief hung.

After the growing awe allowed her mouth to work again,

"Holy friggin' shit."

"Forrest said it was mind-blowing, but I am beyond rocked," Rain stammered.

An enormous gold nugget sat on top. The thing was heavy, as she lifted it out.

"Wow!" was all that could come out of anyone's open mouths for a long time.

"Let's unpack this carefully," Rain finally said.

She could still barely speak.

Words were not adequate.

Two hundred and sixty-five gold American Double Eagles, with a few five dollar and old Middle Eastern coins lined the table.

Behind them, two flat, round five-inch mirrors reflected.

Ornate.

Magical.

Shelby tried on a Spanish ring with a large emerald.

Rain guessed it was the one they found with a metal detector in the Galisteo Basin, which put them there with gold. Historical.

Changes came with that ring.

Dark changes.

Adam held a gold dragon, high up to the light, turning it, admiring.

It was the one from the pictures in *The Thrill of The Chase.*

Bigger in real life.

Iam was holding a jar, filled with gold dust, watching it sparkle.

He blew a bit on them all.

The group was laughing uncontrollably.

"Get it together, ya'll we are being too loud. This all is for a cause. Don't let it infect you," Iam reminded them.

Rain was getting short of breath and took two finely carved jade faces out and walked around Room 16 flushed, pacing, unable to contain her excitement.

She grabbed a pillow and screamed into it gleefully.

Having heard Iam, she tried to calm down but bounced on the bed for a second.

Shelby cried out, "This must be the bracelet Forrest wants back." Twenty-two turquoise disks lined in a row and formed a beautiful bracelet.

It was simple.

The connection to the Turquoise Twins apparent in the energy.

"Shelby, set that over there for me, please. We need it to go to Forrest."

"Sure thing."

Shelby had started counting rubies, "two hundred and fifty-four, nobody's poor!"

Two Ceylon sapphires, eight emeralds and a palmful of small diamonds, were counted.

Two fascinating gold bracelets, pre-Columbian, came out next.

"Ooooo, these are pretty." Shelby decorated her arms.

Iam pulled out an object of power.

It was the Tairona and Sinu quartz, carnelian, jadeite necklace.

A gold frog and a jaguar claw rested in the center.

This was his reason for looking for it.

He was to take this home.

He strode off to the side and sat cross-legged, quietly, holding the necklace.

A small glass jar, with a sealed metal lid was next.

"Oh, let me see that, it is his autobiography," Rain said.

"I want to read it right now."

She started melting the wax.

Absorbed in the story, she let them finish.

"What? This treasure started with some other treasure in that rock?" Rain read.

Fascinated.

Straining to see it with the magnifying glass.

Adam was fishing in the box and pulled out a couple of huge nuggets and many smaller gold pieces.

A pile was mounding.

Forrest had carefully packed the box.

It held more than looked possible.

Forty-two pounds of treasure lay on the table.

The last item was wrapped in black paper and tied in cotton string.

Rain came to attention.

"Be careful with that. Forrest said there was something special in the chest."

"This thing could be dangerous, it looks magical."

A protective circle was formed.

Shelby gingerly untied it.

Rain could hardly believe her eyes and had to blink.

She could only stare.

She felt the tears hit her arm before she knew she was crying.

"That is impossible."

The corner of a paper with "Deed" scrawled on top fell out.

Another paper explained her role as the new Guardian of the Secrets.

There was not a choice.

It had been decided.

The quest taken on.

Rain had succeeded, but was not finished.

Carrying the old Royal bloodlines, gave her access to the magic at San Lazaro.

Rain's training would begin in earnest.

The reality of her dreams to save the planet rested now in her ownership of the ancient information station at San Lazaro.

The four spread out with the treasures, each to return items across Gaia.

Rain went back to New Mexico, alone.

She had a delivery.

Forrest opened his mailbox.

Inside, there was a small, plain, checkbook-size box.

It was wrapped in the Sunday Funnies.

He opened it.

His turquoise bracelet stared at him.

He laughed and laughed.

"Peggy, we are finally free!"

"That girl has no idea what she is taking on, but she must be the one to carry the secrets."

"I did everything I could to get her out of there, but she found my box."

"What Bubba, it has been found?"

"Yes, dear, now I can tell you all about it."

"Remember when I bought the ruins?"

"Wait, somebody found it? You don't care?"

"Honey, I wanted her to find it, now I can pass the weight of the secrets."

"She will not tell she found it, but will be buying my ruins."

Forrest laughed and laughed.

"I do not understand?" Peggy could not help but laugh too.

"What?" she giggled.

"Let me start at the beginning," Forrest said.

CHAPTER XXXIII

IT BEGINS

"When the student is ready the teacher will appear."

Buddha

Inika ran, the wind almost drowned the sound.

She recognized the voice.

She had spent all winter establishing herself as their leader, so was not going to be called or caught.

"Run," she screamed.

"Hey girl, hey girl, Nikka, come here baby," the man cooed.

Something sweet came across her nose.

The winter had been long, it smelled good.

Cautiously she approached.

"That's a good girl, come here, baby, that's my girl."

She called for all of them to follow.

Surrounding the man and the boy, she allowed indulgence.

The bucket of sweet feed quickly was eaten.

He slipped a rope around her neck.

"What a pretty little horse," Rain said.

"She's as wild as they get, She is my favorite," Iam replied.

"She is one of the horses from Plains. They'll give 'em to the right people."

The herd was watching every move.

She reared, purposely missing the man, but knocking him down.

Snickering, she was pleased to see the young stallion watching.

The harsh tones did not change the small victory.

"Hey, hey you, down, down, no!"

She might like him, but a leader now, she had to show her dominance.

The boy, around 14, was timidly standing near.

She could feel the fear and relaxed.

She liked children.

"She is, like, really cool."

"Yeah, look how she's calling the rest of 'em."

"Check it out, she's like the queen, can I touch her?"

"Well, now let's see if she is fixin' to fuss no-more."

"What?"

"Oh, anymore?"

Rain winked.

They were working on grammar.

She had never heard someone who could use a triple negative in conversation, regularly.

Rain loved what Iam had to say, and thought changing the delivery might be useful.

Her own upbringing had been strict with vocabulary and grammatical drills. With foreign languages on both sides, it had been important English was well-spoken and written.

Rain cringed at each, "Ain't never nobody couldn't."

It also was a source of laughter between the two.

They laughed often.

Stephen, blonde, lanky, growing rapidly looked at them studiously.

He had come from New Jersey to stay with his family at the huge ranch in Camas Prairie. He had heard that the well-known horseman, Iam, would be there.

His family had been talking about Iam and a girl he was bringing.

He was bored.

This sounded fun.

The gossip had sparked his interest.

"He wants to bring out some girl."

"A girl?"

"Well, who?"

"She is local, trouble. Remember the Bauer family?"

"Oh heck yeah, that girl?"

"Good-night, what on God's green earth is he doing with her?"

"Or her with him," Jim Knobel thought to himself.

He had seen her a few weeks ago at Buck's.

She had grown up nicely.

His wife caught the look and smacked his arm.

"Hey, you wipe that look off your face, you perv. She is worse trouble now, I hear. "

"Yeah, they say she has gone crazier, hunting some treasure, thinking she can fix things."

He heard rumor of her "work" too.

Was curious.

"Whatever, pass me the beans, babe."

That had been it, Stephen nosy now.

He thought maybe Rain was weird, quiet and really pretty, he daydreamed.

The little horse nearly stepped on him.

Iam had a plane ticket for South America.

It left in one week.

He and Rain spending lots of time before it left.

He felt himself falling for her.

The Jaguar claw necklace and several jade figurines were safely hidden and on the way already.

Separating the travelers from the items had become important.

It had not taken long for Forrest to catch up to them.

Opening his mailbox, a small, rectangular box, wrapped in the recent Sunday Comics laughed at him.

He gingerly opened it.

Lately, he had opened his box to a shredded copy of his book and a degrading message that left a stinky trail for weeks.

He was nervous.

Unsure his job was done.

He wished his words had been written differently.

Once they were written and published, too late.

He really had given it away, and since the trespassing and thievery would expose his lies, he had to just let it be.

Unwrapping the carefully taped box, he lifted the lid away from himself. With a cocked eye, he looked.

Turquoise.

He stared.

His bracelet.

His heart soared.

His stomach sank.

Once he finished laughing.

"I will tell you everything, soon."

He quickly stood.

He almost knocked over Peggy getting to his office.

"Gosh, Bubba, look out."

"Sorry," he kept forward.

Peggy stared open-mouthed.

"Well, well, some spunk." She giggled quietly.

Forrest worked the levers, slipped into his secret tech room and started backtracking and hunting.

Once they had it, the trail had picked back up in Colorado.

He watched as they began to split up the treasure and make plans to distribute and disperse.

His phone rang.

"Mr. Fenn, sir," the agent said, "We have reason to believe your treasure chest has been uncovered, as we previously informed you, the articles within remain under investigation, and if discovered, must be reported."

"Mr. Pitts, sir, I have told you, nobody will find that box, including you."

Forrest angrily hung the phone up.

"Stupid darn government messing with my stuff, again."

Now what.

He sat stumped.

How could he help?

Rain was not supposed to find the treasures until she remembered the whole story.

Forrest figured intervention was involved.

He took out the ancient communication crystal and called the Council.

They were already, of course, working to awaken Rain fully.

Her object, the Jade Frog, was to go to Honduras.

Stolen, originally, then again by Forrest, it held powerful energy.

The FBI wanted it.

Forrest would go to jail, for the rest of his years, if found.

Nobody could prove a thing, without it.

"Oh great, Wise Council, I have failed my mission, the chest has been found, please tell me she was meant to," Forrest spoke, anxiety evident in his wavering voice.

"We have needed to hurry, the distractions were coming too fast, paired with her sick, we stepped in." A deep and soothing voice spoke in his mind, "We gave her the ideas for the last two clues, for Medicine Rock.

"The Frog returned to the base, will activate more awakening.

"Ahomea struggles.

"The residual fogs still drift, but the Planet is holding.

"More and more humans with clear auras and vision are surfacing," the voice spoke.

"There is hope, still, Sagiditis is gone."

While Gaia heals and repairs, regrows, careful tending is needed. Your work is not finished; it has just started. She needs instructions on how to protect the ruins, the mysteries. It all happened differently than Seen."

Forrest gulped.

Sat back with his arms behind his head, closed his eyes for a second.

That girl, Rain, he had met before this life.

Given her instructions then.

Now.

Neither listened to.

Perhaps this life might turn around the Wheel differently, though.

The Light Warriors of the Universe were always on call, ready to help, risking their own safety, time and time again, for Gaia and other planets, at risk.

Rain held high status, but needed to prove herself.

She had been tricked before.

Leading her people astray.

Too gullible.

Too trusting.

Her fault so much has gone wrong.

The guilt within her at the loss and deception, the drive behind her quest.

Letting go of these ancient mistakes, next.

Traveling alone, after spending weeks with Iam, Rain was on edge.

The mysteries of her past unraveling, flashes and images from other times kept her mind rolling in memories.

She barely noticed the surroundings.

Her hunger overtook a dull fog and she stopped in Clark Fork, Idaho, at the Pantry.

While she was inside, a shiny black SUV pulled up beside her car, which she had painted purple and cut a sunroof in.

Three burly men climbed out.

One stayed behind, taking his bulletproof vest off for a second while he changed shirts.

He was irritated and sweaty.

It had been hard to keep up with Reagan Bauer.

She lived in such remote places, never traveled predictably and he had decided she had a sixth sense about their presence and messed with him.

Watching her in her new relationship had him on edge.

As he walked into the Pantry, he saw his men flirting with her at the counter.

It was too much.

"Smith, what is taking you so long?" he snapped.

His colleagues simply stared at him.

Harold Barker, shorter than them all, an attitude to match, was losing it, they all thought.

"Be right out." Smith said.

He towered over Rain, looked her up and down.

"How are you today?"

"Great." She smiled, smelled cop.

Quickly left.

The shiny black, brand new SUV had Texas plates, with no stickers.

Interesting, Rain thought.

She eased onto the road and at Lighting Creek, took a quick right.

The SUV passed without seeing her.

Inside the rig, tension rose.

They all were tired of looking for Forrest Fenn's stolen articles.

Irritated at the crazy trail Rain took them on.

Interested, now that she had been close.

Her energy was contagiously seductive.

She smelled of sandalwood and jasmine, smiled enormously.

Her pictures and watching from afar had not prepared them for the feel of her.

They were aware she was under surveillance for her body rub business, but were after the artifacts not petty crimes.

Rain did not have any treasure on her.

It was on the way South, already.

The team had quickly set a plan in motion to disperse and confuse.

Once uncovered, a flurry of activity to find them had begun.

The week before had been the best week of Rain's life.

She and Iam had spent it together.

Laughing, loving, planning for a future together.

A future world.

They had run from one hot springs to the next in an irregular pattern.

The day verbally started one direction, and physically ended elsewhere.

They took back roads, doubled back.

Stopped at scenic sites where there was no cell coverage.

Every day, a bug scanner was run around the car.

Twice a tracking device found, removed, and placed on another vehicle.

Harold was beyond tense.

There was not a great way to follow her.

The agents suspected the treasure was not in her possession.

Her VW had been carefully searched, as well as her room.

The assignment remained to stay on her.

Where was she?

"Smith, where the hell did she go?"

"I do not know, sir," Smith flushed.

He thought he had been watching closely.

Their eyes had been on her most times.

There had been a corner just before.

He quickly swung the rig around.

They could still see the dust from a car on Rapid Lighting, but the car gone.

Rain was at large, without a tracker on her.

With just enough time, she was back on Highway 200, headed towards Missoula.

She ditched her car in Noxon, picking up a hitchhiker on the way.

The girl had really short bleach blonde hair, seemed edgy and tired.

Rain sensed she needed help, picked her up.

The short drive from Heron to Noxon had Rain convinced this girl did not want more than self-destruction.

She happily dumped the girl at Toby's, grabbed the stylish BMW bike waiting for her in the alley.

She changed into riding clothes, pinning her hair under a long blonde wig.

When the agents caught up to her on the road, they rode by.

Rain saw them, though.

Smiled hugely.

Harold Barker saw the smile out of the corner of his eye.

It nagged him, but he could not pin it.

Rain sighed.

A small victory.

She still had a long way to go.

Her emotions had wavered that day.

She had gotten a text.

A staff member from Spring Creek was dying.

Sandra Hogram had been one of the most feared counselors. When she stormed into a room for group, you knew it would be a long one.

Often the kids were forced to sit for hours until somebody confessed breaking some rule.

Sometimes somebody confessed for them so everyone could leave and just take whatever punishment was doled out.

Maybe a fifteen-mile walk down the Blue Slide, picking up trash.

Perhaps a day digging gravel to fill the road.

Or worse, being put into solitary.

Sandra had been excellent at finding rule breakers, and better at doling the punishments.

Over the years, she had softened, apologized for how controlling and manipulative she had been.

Rain remembered her green eyes flashing around the circle looking to find the culprit who had stolen a gallon of honey from the larder, landing on her.

Rain had squirmed, needed to go to the bathroom, be anywhere but there.

She had not done it, but felt like it.

Rain got the message Sandra was filling up with tumors.

She had gone to the MD with the same symptoms Rain had, but went for conventional treatment.

It had not worked.

Rain figured with how stubborn Sandra was, she would have made it.

She felt the tears, hot on her face, with the cool air from the bike teasing them dry.

A moment of fear crept in.

What if she really was not healthy yet?

Rain banished the thought, and sent out a positive one.

"I am perfectly healthy, strong, free and powerful, thank you Creator."

Sad for Sandra and her family, Rain hoped she would pass quickly.

Pressing on, she revved the bike through the curves, needing to pay attention to the details of the road, she forgot her sorrow and rode fast and hard South.

CHAPTER XXXIV

THE SWITCH

"The Universal Mind contains all knowledge. It is the potential ultimate of all things. To It, all things are possible. To us, as much as we can conceive, according to law. Should all the wisdom of the Universe be poured over us, we should yet receive only that which we are ready to understand."

Ernest Holmes
The Science of Mind

The week before had been the most intense week of planning.

Chaos and unpredictability, the friends of the team.

Aware eyes were waiting to know where the treasure went, scenes were created to implant the wrong scent.

After dropping Shelby and Adam in Salt Lake, Rain stopped to see Andy.

He answered his door sleepy eyed and surprised.

Rain had gotten good enough to be off his radar.

He had been really busy with the increased pressure to dismantle a couple prostitution rings, out of touch with his favorite suspect.

She was wearing a short black wig and dark, tight fitting clothes.

She looked amazingly alive.

It had taken him a second to recognize her.

"Shit, what are you doing here?"

It was his office he used as a cover.

"I have something for you."

"Oh?" His interest stirred on a few levels.

She still got to him.

He shifted uncomfortably.

Rain saw and grinned a half-cocked maniacal grin.

"We are way past me showing you that, mister," she teased.

"Get in here before someone sees you." He almost gently pulled her into his small, dimly lit office.

Andy shut and locked the door.

He looked her over as she un-pinned her hair from the wig.

Long red, wavy hair tumbled out.

He smelled a wave of her scent.

Fresh, sweaty, full of danger, wind, flowers and secret places.

"What do you have," he snapped.

Too aware of her.

"Be nice, agent man, or I turn around," she snapped back.

"Alright, I am sorry, things are stressful lately, I miss you. Can I see them?" He grabbed for her.

Rain, angry now, gave his hand a quick but hard backhanded pop.

"Ouch."

"Mind your manners."

"I thought you missed me," he sulked.

"Do you want to see or not?" she demanded.

His interest was peaked.

She was not there for sex.

"Reagan, show me." He used her real name and his best agent voice.

"Nah, I already mailed it back to Forrest already, anyway."

He paled.

Took a minute to just stare at her.

"Seriously?"

"Yes, I found it."

"Yeah, whatever, now what do you really want, I am busy," Andy said.

Rain reached into her pocket.

It was small, easy to conceal.

A gold double Eagle.

"For you." She tossed it to him.

He caught it.

His mouth hung open.

He said nothing.

The room still.

Frozen.

"Close your mouth. There is much more for you, if you help."

"I need a smokescreen." Rain studied his face carefully.

Emotions rolled across.

"Where is the rest?" His eyes sparkled.

"I want to see." He sounded like a small child.

"No way, we are being fol-lowed. The box is split up, traveling with Rainbow Road Warriors. By now, most of it has left the country, or has been divided to help the com-munity," Rain assured him.

"But I have the Jade Frog. It is going home to the ruins. Back to the tomb it was stolen out of. Your pals are on my ass, but their leader is a ninny and loses me." Rain giggled at the end of her sentence, hardly able to finish.

He struggled to digest it all.

Reagan found his treasure.

Andy had not expected her in-terest when he shared the quest.

He had been glad to have someone to share hunt stories with, but had not thought she would be seriously after the box.

Not his treasure.

Reagan Bauer had it.

He felt his face flush.

What choice did he have.

"What else did you save?"

"You will like it," she purred.

He softened, realizing his situation.

"So, when do you need the screen and for how long?" he asked.

"Tomorrow night. Give me at least twelve hours ahead of them. It is the team arriving about, well, now." Rain pulled back his curtain, showed him the standard FBI rig sliding in a few spots down from her now purple VW.

She could feel the tension oozing.

"All right, but when do I get to have my prize?" he asked, looking parched.

"Andy, hon, I am in love," Rain soothed.

"With me, I know," he teased.

"No, you know we were never in love. I just reminded you of what is already in you, doll. You know I love you, care, and want you well, but a secret relationship does not do it for me pumpkin. I found my match." Rain quickly hugged him. "If it works, go to Lava Hot Springs. I left you something there, already. I will text you where, if I make it," Rain said.

He swallowed a lump watching her leave.

He wondered about this match of hers, he almost felt sorry for the man.

She tucked her disguise away, emerging as herself, climbed in her car.

The new tracker attached to the VW was working.

She had left it on, parking her car earlier, going in to eat.

She had climbed out the bathroom window as a different girl, crossed the lot to the tall glass office building.

Too long in the bathroom, Harold Barker had knocked.

Gotten no response.

Realized quickly the girl with short black hair he had seen cross the lot earlier, had probably been Rain.

Her car was still there, but he decided to drive and look.

She could not be far.

Rain was just across the lot, then, going to see Andy.

Harold spotted her.

"There she is," Harold said, spilling his coffee.

His colleagues rolled their eyes at each other.

Harold was getting intense about Reagan Bauer.

Obsession was next.

He had recently been on leave.

He had gotten too involved in a suspect's life.

Ruined three years of undercover work.

This assignment was a true test if he was ready.

He was showing cracks.

Smith had been told to monitor and report.

He took note of the reaction.

Felt his respect dip.

All of them thought Reagan was interesting.

They enjoyed reading her history.

Envied the agents on the other teams, after her.

This assignment seemed superfluous to Smith.

She obviously was playing games, wasting their time and money.

Smith would bet millions the artifacts were already gone.

Smith knew what the Jade Frog would do, if it made it home.

He had been part of the FBI's team to recover artifacts for twenty-seven years.

The Jade Frog had gone missing from the base it sat on, when Forrest Fenn arrived in the jungles of Honduras.

Forrest had entered the tomb of one of the most powerful shamans ever.

He walked out with the frog, leaving the rest of his life in the tomb.

A chain of events would cascade.

He had not known what he was taking or how long it would take to undo what he had done.

The people it belonged to were looking.

"The girl, she has it, it comes home, our place can be returned, celebrate, celebrate!" The cries surrounded the village, deep in the recesses of a Honduran jungle.

Ruins surrounded the village lost in time, far from the advances of technology.

The ruins told stories of invasion, traveling North, setting up new homes, hiding powerful magic in objects and stones, and of a new time coming soon.

"Does the man with the hat follow her?" asked a woman.

"No, not this time, he has given his power to the girl, but others follow her, we must watch and help. She is to join the Frog on His journey and bring Him home." The Shaman spoke in a trance.

He stayed in a seated meditation, watching, waiting.

The woman hung her head.

She had hoped the man might return.

He had promised.

She had waited.

A joke in the village at first, now sad.

Several watched as she hobbled back to her hut.

By now, they all knew, it would be a few days before anyone saw her.

Headed North on I-15, when she reached Idaho, she sent a text.

"LOL, TY, check the Owl."

One week before, Rain and Iam had spent one night at Lava Hot Springs Inn.

In the replica of the chest, found early in the search, she left several diamonds, a few rubies, a handful of gold nuggets, the dark mirror and a note in tiny lettering.

"Dear Andy, thank you for all the lessons, as I reflect into myself and see you, I know now what IF means, you are perfect just like you are, do good with this. All the Love the World has to you, Rainy Day."

She hoped he would know what

it meant, had unscrewed the water-bearing Owl and left the chest, in a small watertight bag, inside the belly for him to figure out.

Lolo had been amazing.

A different experience than the first few times they were there.

It had been a friendship.

A quest for treasure.

Quickly the similarities in personality had been noticed.

They had become inseparable.

Age was no matter.

They reflected a twin image and had both asked for the perfect partner or none.

Each very different, hard to call a particular label.

Native-minded, a dash of hippy with a huge side of cowboy and at times intense.

After she left the treasure for Andy, she wrapped herself in Iam's arms in the pool.

He floated her on her back, spun her in a slow circle.

The stars dancing with them, time suspended.

It was not the first time he had asked her to be his wife.

In other lives, they ruled together, drove empires to glory and helped hide it when that time came.

They had watched as the other had been persecuted for their belief in the good of Gaia and her magic the last time.

"Rainy Day, you bring sunshine to my world, please say you will walk with me in this life as my wife."

"Wife? I thought you did not like all that?"

"Well, a cute handfasting now, darlin', stay out of the system, please say you will, before I die right here?" He looked worried.

"Of course I will, I cannot imagine a better partner, I love you so much."

"You too, my baby, I love you too." He softly cried and held her.

"Thank you, God, thank you, I have a wonderful woman to love who loves me and all my weirdness."

"You gotta be weird to be in my world!" Rain kissed him until she needed air.

They held onto one another in the pools until the staff came out to tell them it was time to close.

Not liking parting, they had needed to.

She tried not to miss him or worry.

Only send good thoughts, she reminded herself.

Rain had several more stops.

After a crazy drive north, and a quick flight south, she was on her way to New Mexico.

Kieran had gone home.

Arguing with the park ranger had cost him some time and all of his funds. She was flying South from Santa Fe, so an extra stop would not hurt.

Rain saved him a few coins and small gems.

She knocked.

He paled when he answered.

After a long moment.

"I am sorry."

"Hey, it all works out, I guess

we had to go there one last time."

He looked relieved.

"Hey, what are doing here, if you are not here to, you know." He flushed.

Rain laughed.

"I found it."

"You are joking. I really thought maybe it was a huge joke, the whole thing." He did not look like he thought it was a good joke.

He looked ill.

Pulling out a small black velvet drawstring from under her clothes, Rain held it up.

"For you, and all of the lifetimes we have learned together. I love you my Brother. My wish is to let you go so I can marry Iam. He's asked me."

"What? Who is Ian?"

"No, Iam, never-mind, he is amazing, he reminds me of you when you settle down years from now. He is super kind, sensitive, caring, strong and he helped me find the Chroma."

Kieran was looking in his bag, looking shocked and confused.

"Wow, where was it? Where is the rest of it? What are you doing now? Whoa, Reagan, this is freaking me out." He paled, sat.

"Hey, I just don't have time right now."

"Do me a favor, though."

Rain detailed out the plan to get on the plane South in a few days.

She hugged him.

Said goodbye.

He did what she asked.

He made a few calls to friends.

One friend had been waiting for this call.

"She did it. We have no choice now, the Power of Old will be re-

turned, the People will See and Know again."

"Start the clock."

A chime, resonated deeply across the Universe and it lined up to wait, watch and keep the last threads of hope.

The planning had worked.

Gaia would live.

Her people again in harmony with the right tune.

Rainy Day, Reagan Bauer, had been many in lifetimes, this one she was to bring this Awakening, remembering the past lives, the past defeats and lessons.

The answers were inside her all along.

They came in notes and music, floating timelessly.

"It is simple, just let go, it is all Love, all Light, darkness is but an illusion of your mind, which is diseased, but can be cured, let go, let go, AHOMEA." Rain heard this song deeply within.

Next was the meeting with Forrest.

He had contacted her, finally.

"Rain, we need to discuss the ruins. I have some people who want to meet you. You will have to be very careful to get rid of your tail." Forrest went on to explain where and when.

It was tomorrow.

She was to go to the feed store and cafe on the Turquoise Trail.

Someone was driving her.

Rain was about to find out who she was and meet the Council.

Iam successfully made it to

Colombia.

He had sent word.

The Kogi Indians were thrilled to get the ancient final chief's necklace back.

It had come from the Lost City, Buritaca.

It had been a Tairona custom to bury all of a chief's possessions.

Haqueros had poached many of the items believed to hold strong magic that only the Chiefs could control.

When dead, all items must remain buried or the Universal flow would be disrupted, turn dark.

The stolen articles had to be reburied.

If returned to the open, only chaos remained.

The team had gathered as much as they could identify to be returned to the rightful places.

It was unfortunate that governments all over the world wanted control.

The Rainbow gathering, though chaotic that year had been a great place to blend in and hide from the agents.

Her tribe engulfed and surrounded, keeping her friends well occupied in the parking lot, before entering the Temple of the Gathering space.

Rainy Day found lots of good folks she knew.

She had lived in so many places, it was hard to call a particular camp Home.

She mingled everywhere.

Spreading the good news and wealth.

She found Caterpillar, from Asheville, N.C. on the third.

He took a load East.

Shelby Sky worked with the Utah tribe.

Adam knew several International tribes, so was able to spread news, treasure and articles to return to Europe.

News spread fast.

The prophecies were coming true.

The Rainbows were going to do it.

Something was wrong though.

A last ditch effort to disrupt the Family.

Many held onto the Light to keep the rest safe.

Three had died at the Gathering.

A tragedy unheard of.

Tickets had been issued right and left.

Dissension in the "leaderless" was happening.

Though the ships were gone, the Light holding, the Dark Twin still held court, until all the items went home.

Shadows attacked thoughts, Enlightenment was no longer an option for Earth, it was mandatory for survival.

Rain sat in quiet meditation all day July Fourth.

She prayed for the Family of Light to continue the mission in force, to awaken to beauty of the Now.

She begged hearts to be filled with Love.

"Would you be could you Be Love, say something." Bob echoed in her mind when her thoughts drifted to the negativity happening around her.

Visualizing Love and Light filling the Universe, the Earth being a conduit.

She stayed grounded.

The next day, she had finished her work.

She took the long hike out, and was met with agents in the lot.

They followed her on a long loop through Salt Lake, Hot Springs, Sandpoint and then back South again.

Her VW had thousands of miles and a couple quick paint jobs.

She was tired.

Sleeping hard for ten hours after her long drive to Santa Fe.

Though under their eyes, Rain had done it.

She just needed to get by them in the morning so she could make it to the feed store in time.

She was at the KOA, not too far from Santa Fe.

Her dreams were wild.

A healer came and pulled a snake out of her.

It hissed and lunged at her, black, ugly.

The healer told her to seal it out of her belly.

The snake was angry.

Gone, but able to still infect thoughts until the items went home, Shankar struggled to get to Rain.

They had ninety days to work or the Serpents would be back.

Opening the chest bought time.

The work still had to be done.

The team was well on the way.

All disguised and well-padded in Family.

Hope and motivation to save Gaia, the switch turned on, Rainbow Family all over whispered that the prophecies about them were true.

Through their thoughts, actions, deeds and words they were warriors of the Light, here to Fight.

Her alarm vibrated under her pillow at 3:45 a.m.

She was to sneak out the back window and be on the side of the road exactly one mile at 4:30 a.m.

Groggy for just a few minutes, the excitement woke her up.

Rain slipped out, unnoticed.

Walked briskly down the road.

It was chilly that morning, she walked fast and huddled in her sweatshirt.

They knew she had done it before they found her at the designated spot.

They always saw.

A gentle-looking man with a beard drove a powder blue Mini Cooper with tinted windows.

She recognized him from dreams that recurred.

"Are you ready, do you hear me? " he asked her in her dreams.

He did again, without his mouth moving.

Rain heard.

"Yes, my Brother."

"Namaste."

The drive was short, feeling stretched out in time.

A surreal and wavy feeling overcame Rain.

Time began to meld.

She was remembering.

She sat in Council.

Arguments erupted over how to handle the invaders.

How to handle the egos and new quest for power that was infecting the long-standing peaceful people of Gaia was debated hotly.

For the first time ever, the people of Atlantis were divided.

The first phase of the Serpent invasion had begun.

Seers were visualizing the current state of Gaia, afraid.

They saw what Gold Fever did.

The infection had already begun.

The Council decided to hide the leaders, wipe memories until now, bury the cities and power objects, and split the Tribe into different places on the planet.

The objects with the highest Magic were encoded and keyed with a complicated series to unlock them.

Only ancient blood could access the mysteries.

Warriors were sent to train for multiple lifetimes on Gaia.

Ready at this time to take Her back.

Rain had made a mistake and trusted an infected person centuries before.

Several hundred who had followed her perished before reaching their new home.

The guilt had stayed with her throughout lifetimes.

She punished herself.

The souls punished her in each life that she returned, suspicious of her bright energy.

Souls remembered, even if consciousness would not allow it up front in the brain.

It was time to forgive.

She had loved them, which was why she had been misled.

Gullible and trusting like most simple and compassionate beings.

She punished herself in each life and took on huge challenges for her soul to overcome.

The only thing left was for her to forgive herself.

She had done the best she could.

She made it to this point and was ready to take her position in the changes to come.

Magic had foreseen the challenges, obstacles and outcome of victory.

The mirrored shadow always possible, but hope always remained that the People would awaken again.

Magic could return and the Mother Dragon able to breathe her healing fires across the land.

CHAPTER XXXV

THE COUNCIL

"If we wish a certain good, we must instill into our
minds a realization of this specific good and then---
As this idea is the mold we place in mind--it will be
filled by the substance necessary for the complete
manifestation of that good in our lives."

Ernest Holmes
The Science of Mind

Time's ravages had not changed
the meeting room.

It rested outside the dimensions
imposed on the rest.

A portal was inside the ruins at
San Lazaro.

After a quick hello, Rain, Forrest, Dago and another man she recognized, drove the last bumpy bit
past the gates.

Forrest had given her the gate
codes, to punch in.

The place was hers.

It felt strange.

She had not been back yet.

Not that long before they had
trespassed to get the chest.

Now she typed in the code.

Standing with Forrest and the
rest watching the sun finish rising.

"So, you are ready, Rain?" Dago
telepathically asked her.

"Yes." The response felt thick
and slow, but she squeaked it out.

Dago heard and nodded to the rest.

"Let's go."

Medicine Rock held the portal into the meeting chambers.

The altar a lever.

Holding onto each other, a flash of light, a sensation of being dragged under a wave, and a pulling tug, then they were in the room.

The air felt thicker, a desert bending it.

It smelled delicious.

Familiar.

Yet, hard to remember.

She felt the connection, though.

Recognized the faces, the feelings.

She knew she was home.

A stir occurred as multiple Light Bodies surrounded her.

"Everyone, we are all glad to finally hold our Sister again, but we have serious work to do still, it is not over yet." Dago spoke with gentle authority.

The crowd moved towards a round table, each taking their places in the thirteen council seats.

The rest encircled.

Ready to listen.

Rain had not sat in her chair for many lifetimes.

Once all in place.

The Wheel lit, energy lines visible and views, visions fell across the table.

Rain saw Iam in South America, being greeted enthusiastically.

Shelby in North America, dispersing wealth.

Adam in Europe spreading change and hope.

She saw all the People smiling and hopeful.

Gaia greening and growing.

Shankar had waited patiently for this moment.

The dream had been a warning.

A small sting and this beast had grown in her.

Rain paled, clutched her belly and screamed.

The snake emerged, leaving Rain drained.

It attacked.

Prepared, though, a trap had already been set for the creature.

Once out.

Rain's vision cleared the rest of the way.

She saw who she was.

Who she had been all along.

Barely conscious, she raised her hands and let the energy grow.

She threw this at the snake.

Weak, but effective, enough of a gap in the attack for the rest to step in.

Just as she passed all the way out, Rain saw victory.

It had been a risk and a last ditch effort to get in.

A bad decision on the enemy's part.

Gaia could finally be free.

Shankar was dead after centuries of lurking and destroying.

A long and often invisible battle finally won.

Peace restored.

The crystals in Gaia active, returned to the correct frequency.

Universal flow in perfect balance.

The Mirrors reflected inwardly, really Seeing.

Visions and dreams harmonious.

Human kind was no longer enslaved.

Returned to a magical state of bliss and balance.
Bells chimed and Angels sang.
The big bang.

"The Brain is wider than the Sky -
For put them side by side -
The one and the other will contain
With ease - And You - beside."
Emily Dickinson
Poem 632

Once Shankar was destroyed, Magic and Dragon's Breath was used to clean Gaia from the pollution and negativity.
Old ways of simplicity became how it was again.
The People knew they had been tricked, but had no shame.
Deep inside the Light within always understood, it just was.
The mess humanity had allowed was wiped clean.
Creator granting another opportunity on the spin of the Wheel.
We had chosen wisely, this time.
Lessons of Old and striving towards healing, magic and resting in Stillness kept the chaos away.
Humanity able to fulfill the destiny set up for us to chose.
Darkness cried as the shadow of the Mirror reflected only Light.
A festival, the Portal Festival, had been planned the year before to gather and celebrate the new paradigm.
Once the team was successful, everyone was to meet back in Lolo Hot Springs, August first.

Rain was the first one there.
The campgrounds were empty for there being a festival the next day.

Rain's stomach lurched.
Where was everyone?
She remembered though, they had won already, but just needed to get everyone together for a focused meditation.
Several activations were planned.
The wealth to be distributed more.
Each piece of treasure was to start a planned community with sustainable farming and shared land responsibility.
They would all be linked, and people to travel, teach, build all over the world.
Rain waited, sitting quietly under a tree, at her camp in the back, looking at the rock formation that pointed a big one.
"We are all one."
It was the perfect place to end the story.
Ahomea was awake and ready to take Her planet back once and for all.
Her children had asked for truth, peace, harmony and a return of the Old ways.
She heard the cry.
Watched the battle in her half slumber.
Heart soaring with hope.
They had not forgotten after all.
Structures were going up and the Tribe was filtering in funky cars and outfits.
You could tell the Family was there.
Flags, sparkles, art and bright people began to dot the fields.
People were laughing and smiling.
Everyone helped to set up and excitement coursed the air.

They had won.

Lifetimes of lies, defeat and misery were done.

The people held Her again.

Gaia breathed slower as She knew that they loved Her as much as She loved them.

Several Portals were formed and lifetimes of information channeled to all willing to hear.

Workshops and music that lasted all night had the adults playing hard and having fun, ready for the expansion.

Rain closed her eyes and saw the whole wheel of time spinning before her, gates allowing her to look in.

She saw lifetimes of defeat and people selling her out to the system.

She let this pain course through her as she remembered all of them in the beginning of time, together, just like this.

Then she let the pain go with the dance.

The whole Tribe energetically knew they were to hold one another in the light, so each could remember their roles.

Each had pieces of the puzzle, the lost library within the ancient codes of their souls.

The information was released into the consciousness of all the People.

Destinies forever on course with Higher Purpose.

The prophecies fulfilled.

With their good intent and visions of a better world, The People of the Crystalline Energy Matrix, had plugged back in.

Chaos moved into a still point, while the wheel of time rested.

They all danced wildly and freely in light up colors, loving each other, doing the dance together.

The weight lifted off the Bearers.

Those who See and Feel, could be Seen and Felt too.

Knowers confirmed within, that the Truth bringers could do it.

They had.

Guides and Angels had been called in to protect, serve and record all that occurred within the gathering.

The message was sent to Mother God and Father God that the codes had been activated, the healing could begin.

During the festival, Rain and a few others circulated seeds of treasure and hope for a people who had for so long struggled and been lied to.

Abundance for all.

Instructions to seed communities that people could live and offer their talents to trade for living.

These communities would be Worldwide and be available to travelers.

Permanent festival grounds were to be built sustainably, offering abundance to all.

Abundance of heart.

Abundance of soul.

Without worry and stress and without being a part of the system.

Though never organized before, a decision had been made to allow an official record of those being in the Family of Light.

All documents of identification with the System destroyed and chosen Names recorded.

All evidence of Reagan Bauer, her birth family in this life, destroyed.

She was Family of Light Number 1371, from the first original circle, before time, related to All, Renegade Warrior of Light, her job was a mixture of all, special, because she was all. She Saw, Felt, Knew, brought Truth and Wove Light webs together.

Rain was an ancient Dancer.

One of the most special of the Atlantean race.

They wove time together.

Held the Tree of Life upon their backs, carrying the weight and seeing the pain.

Her major obstacle was struggling in believing the People would not let her down again.

Sell her for a bag of silver, burn her, drown, hang, stick her on a cross, for loving them.

The greed disease gone, Rain just trusted, when the time came to do the dance in the Portal, she was ready to let them hold her again.

She saw the Wheel, saw her guides, saw back in time.

She remembered this same place.

Now they could begin.

With the treasure safely in the folds of Family, her work to spread light a reality, Rain went home to Iam, who waited patiently for her to arrive.

THE CHROMA

RESOURCES for the TREASURE HUNTER

The Thrill of the Chase website is the foremost platform for all news of the Forrest Fenn phenomena. Filmmaker and treasure hunter Dal Neitzel is the dedicated publisher.
www.dalneitzel.com

Collected Works Bookstore and Coffeehouse in Santa Fe is an easy resource for all books and maps in the Forrest Fenn universe.
www.CollectedWorksBookstore.com

Tired of the modern world? Want to turn back the clock? The Green River Rendezvous in Pinedale, Wyoming is always on the second full weekend of July. This is a good time event for all pioneer women and mountain men.
www.pinedaleonline.com/RendezvousDays.HTM

The Chroma author Ansley Ray has website for her treasure hunting adventures.
www.elihsun13.wordpress.com

Treasure impresario Forrest Fenn offers a fascinating website of the history and artifacts of the Old West.
www.oldsantafetradingco.com

While treasure hunting, author Ansley Ray recommends the Days Inn Thermopolis in Thermopolis, Wyoming. She says, "It's pet friendly!" The hotel is near the Wyoming Dinosaur Center and the world's largest hot mineral spring. 115 E Park Street, Thermopolis, WY 82443; Phone: 307-864-3131

Santa Fe Visitors Bureau
www.santafe.org
Phone: 800-777-2489

Yellowstone National Park
www.nps.gov/yell/index.htm
Phone: 307-344-7381

The Rainbow Family of Living Light is a loose-knit group of free-spirited individuals who are dedicated to the practice of peace, love, equality and ecology. Every year, around the Fourth of July weekend, a Rainbow Gathering is held in an American forest. There is no official website, but a simple internet search provides much.
"When the earth is ravaged and the animals are dying, a new tribe of people shall come unto the earth from many colors, classes, creeds, and who by their actions and deeds shall make the earth green again. They will be known as the warriors of the Rainbow"
~ Old Native American Prophecy

About the Author

Ansley Ray is the author of *The Chroma, Boy in Nature* and *Heron Hills*.

Raised in the South, Ray has been living in Northwest Montana for twenty years, loving the outdoors and all of its adventures and treasures.

Photo: www.BrettColvinPhotography.com

THE

CHROMA

HOUSE

www.GordyGrundy.com